The God Slayer

The God Slayer

Roy Chester

ROBERT HALE · LONDON

© Roy Chester 2010
First published in Great Britain 2010

ISBN 978-0-7090-9113-4

Robert Hale Limited
Clerkenwell House
Clerkenwell Green
London EC1R 0HT

www.halebooks.com

2 4 6 8 10 9 7 5 3 1

Typeset in 10½/14pt Palatino
by Derek Doyle & Associates, Shaw Heath
Printed in Great Britain by the MPG Books Group, Bodmin and King's Lynn

To
Oliver

PROLOGUE

Prague, Bohemia–Moravia: June, 1942.

Reinhard Heydrich was dead. Assassinated in the Prague suburb of Holesovice with the help of Czech resistance fighters.

And the reprisals had already started.

The night was black, the air as thick and heavy as velvet, as the figure left the Pinkas synagogue and glided along the walkway fringing the old Jewish cemetery. Then he heard the noise of an engine and stopped, watching the road on the other side of the cemetery. He gasped as he saw the covered troop carrier pull up and the soldiers pour out. In the dim glow from the headlamps he saw the uniforms of the men, and felt the rush of fear.

They were SS. Reinhard Heydrich's own troops out to avenge the death of their leader.

Quickly, the man slipped into the graveyard. He glanced down at the blanket he was carrying. Satisfied that the object under it was still safe, he moved further into the interior of the cemetery. Some of the ornately carved headstones appeared to have been crushed together in a confused jumble, and as the man knelt for a moment in the shadow of a tall monument he felt the weight on his soul of the thousands and thousands of Jews buried here.

As he watched, a second troop carrier pulled into the street outside. And this time the shock was like ice in his stomach as he heard the sound. The fierce barking of the dogs as their SS handlers began to ready them to search the street. And the man cursed as he thought of Ari out there, moving in to make the rendezvous.

Did the SS know something? Were they laying a trap? Or was this simply a random search? The thoughts ran around the man's mind as he tried to work out an escape strategy.

Then he heard a shot, and the dogs went berserk. In the shadows hanging around the headlights he saw that an SS officer was down on the road; suddenly a searchlight mounted on top of the cab of one of the transports cut the night apart. And almost at once another shot rang out and the searchlight shattered into fragments.

The troops moved up the street, employing well tested 'search and find' techniques. And the man realized what Ari was doing. Once he'd seen the trucks he was trying to draw the soldiers away. But seconds later several shots were fired, and a terrible screaming sound broke the silence of the night as the dogs sated their bloodlust.

'Here.' The voice was so low that the man nearly missed it, then a shadow emerged from behind one of the gravestones.

'Ari's out there and—' The words were cut off as the man felt a hand over his mouth.

'Ari's dead.' The words were harsh, cold even. 'The treasure cannot be allowed to fall into the hands of the SS. So you must take Ari's place and move it to the next rendezvous point.'

'Where's that?' he asked. For security reasons the man only knew about his own part in the escape.

'Go to the main square in Mala Strana. There you will see a bakery with a metal sign of a wheatsheaf over the door. Next to the shop is an alleyway that leads into a small courtyard with a tree in the centre. Someone will be waiting for you under the tree. I will try to distract the SS, but remember, you are not supposed to be out in the streets. So stay close to the shadows. Shalom.'

The figure melted away into the night.

Leeds, England: November, 2004:

It was cold. Cold and dark and damp.

If he stretched his arms upwards he could feel the trapdoor. It was bolted on the outside, but he was strong enough now to smash it open. But it hadn't always been like that. When he was younger, being shut away in the box for hours on end was a terrifying experience. But it was drummed into him that it was a necessary punishment for the sin of defying God.

And the God of his father was a harsh, unforgiving God. A God who demanded total obedience from the boy. From the whole family. That had been beaten into the children from the time when they were very young.

As he crouched in the hole, the boy felt consumed by guilt. Guilt because he'd never stood up to his father. Never challenged him. Not even now when he was old enough, strong enough, to defy him. Physically and mentally. But he remained a coward. Even though his sister and his mother suffered terribly at the hands of his father. And over the years the guilt had built up. Tearing him apart inside a dark prison.

The situation had got worse as the time approached for him to leave home for university where he would finally be free of his father's tyranny. The incident that had sparked off this latest punishment was typical of what had been happening over the last few months. His father had found some imaginary fault with him, and to calm him down the boy had allowed himself to be shut away in the box. There wasn't much space in there, and to ease the cramp he was beginning to feel he shifted his position on the damp earthen floor and wondered how long his father would keep him down there.

Then he heard the noise from above, sharp angry voices raised in argument. Voices that suddenly changed into screams. He crashed into the trapdoor with his shoulder and felt the bolts snap off the wood as the door burst free.

The scene inside the garage was straight out of a nightmare. The screams came from his sister. She was crouching in a corner against a metal bench, as his father raised a leather belt above his head.

The boy hurled himself across the floor and crashed into his father, sending him flying. Then he beat him to a pulp.

1

The night air was warm, filled with the scents of flowers from the garden at the rear of the synagogue, a peaceful enclave carved out of the surrounding streets.

But the peace was an illusion, shattered abruptly as the police escort led Fiona Nightingale around a corner into a narrow alley between high brick walls. After ducking under the scene-of-crime tape drawn across the entrance to the alley she went through a pair of high gates and entered the area at the rear of the synagogue. This was a place of frenzied activity filled with noise and bright lights and people. And the smell on the air was different, changed now to the rich cloying odour of death.

But behind the apparent chaos, there was order. The SOCOs, alien life forms in their hooded anti-contamination suits and masks, were searching the area; photographing the scene with still and video cameras, and collecting evidence. Numbered yellow markers, used to indicate the position of anything of interest, were scattered around the search grid. And, at the centre of everything, was the blue plastic tent with the bright lights inside it.

Fiona was logged into the site record by a WPC, and given white anti-contamination gear. She left her handbag with the constable, and slipped on the protective gear; body suit with hood, plastic overshoes and gloves, and a face mask. Then she was escorted to the tent along a safe pathway designated to protect the rest of the crime scene.

With her mask on, Fiona stopped at the entrance to the tent and looked inside. The hooded figure of a man was kneeling in front of something on the ground. He looked up as he sensed Fiona's presence, then stood and walked across to her, pulling off his mask as stepped outside the tent.

'Fiona.' The white suit seemed to enhance the ebony of his skin.

'Gary.' Fiona removed her own mask and smiled. She'd worked with DCI Falcon in the past and they'd become friends.

'Thanks for coming so promptly.' Falcon seemed happy to breathe in the outside air. 'But I know you like to see the scene of a crime in place.'

It was true. She'd learned early in her career that getting the feel of a crime scene in situ was very important.

'So, what have we got?' she asked.

'I'm sorry I couldn't go into detail over the phone, but I wanted to make certain that the scene was secured and scenes of crime were here in force before I did anything else. But essentially, a man's been murdered by having a lance with a dragon banner on it driven into his chest. Oh yes, and one other thing. A sign's been carved into the victim's flesh with a knife.'

'A sign?'

'Yes, the Star of David.'

2

The major incident room was already coming to life. White-coated technicians were firing up the computers and digital display screens, checking the phone lines and setting out cardboard witness statement and evidence boxes.

Assistant Chief Constable Mallory was waiting on the dais at the far end of the open-plan room. Fiona smiled as he came forward. His face was craggy, and his nose looked as if it been broken more than once; a legacy of his days as rugby league player. But to Fiona's surprise, he was dressed in a well-cut blue blazer, instead of his usual comfortable, but strictly old-fashioned, sports coat. He was even wearing a patterned tie. Obviously, Fiona thought, his bride-to-be had decided to take his dress sense in hand.

'Fiona.' He shook her hand. 'I won't say it's good to see you again, because we both might live to regret that. But thanks for getting here so promptly. Now, let's sit down and see what we've got here.'

He led the way to one of the two glass-fronted offices at the far end of the dais. Inside, a wooden laminate desk with a computer terminal on the surface filled the centre of the floor, and the wall space was taken up with filing cabinets and rows of steel shelving, empty now. They sat down in red plastic bucket chairs which were arranged around a low table under a window overlooking the main floor of the dais.

'Before we kick off, can I ask you for your first thoughts at the crime scene?' Mallory asked.

'OK.' Fiona took a small notebook out of her handbag and turned to a page which contained a drawing of the scene as well as notes. 'When I looked at the totality of the surroundings my first thought was that the figure of the murdered man in the tent looked as if it had been arranged. Set there according to some arcane instructions. Squatting cross-legged on the ground, arms pulled behind his back. The lance was lying on the floor, but one of the SOCOs told me that when they arrived it had been driven into the ground beside the body. The victim's clothes had been removed from his upper body, and the sign had been carved into the skin of his chest. At first, I didn't understand why the body hadn't toppled over, but Gary pointed out it was leaning back against a pile of rubble. And my original impression still stands. This was a very carefully staged murder scene with strongly violent overtones, witnessed by driving the lance into the victim's lower body and carving the sign on his chest.'

'What did you mean when you said it was set-up following arcane instructions?'

'It was the way the victim's body seemed to have been posed, exposing the sign cut into his chest. It just struck me as showing all the signs of some kind of sacrificial ritual.'

'Thank you, we can come back to those first impressions later. But let's bring you up to speed now.'

'Who called in the incident?' Fiona asked.

'A witness.' Falcon smiled for the first time that night. 'I didn't tell you at the scene because I wanted you to gather your impressions without any preconceptions. But we have a witness, a Phillip Abelson, who saw the whole thing. In accordance with best practice we took a preliminary witness statement at the scene because, as you know, memory can distort the facts later. Then we brought him back here, and DI Dan Logan started to conduct an in-depth interview. But Abelson's an old man and he was pretty shaken-up by what he'd seen. So much so that Dan called in the duty doctor who thought the witness might have had a mild heart attack and sent him to the A&E at St Martins; they're keeping him in overnight for observation. But at least we got the preliminary statement.'

'And what did it say?'

'Phillip Abelson had been in the synagogue going over some accounts with his friend Rabbi Joseph Caton. Apparently, the two of them are joint treasurers for the fund that's been set-up to pay for the alterations to the area at the rear of the synagogue. Anyway, when they'd finished tonight, the rabbi stayed behind and said he wanted to sit for a while on a bench in the garden. It seems he did this a lot, used to say the peace and quiet let him think. In fact, the rabbi himself donated one of the benches in the garden, and he's one of the prime movers behind the extension plans.'

'What exactly are they doing behind the synagogue?' Fiona asked. 'Because the area where the body was found is like a building site.'

'The land at the back used to be split into two, a garden section and a car-park. But recently, the synagogue has acquired a plot of wasteland nearby and plans to turn that into a car-park, leaving all the land at the rear to be a garden. And, at the moment, yes, half of it is like a building site while the old Tarmacadam surface gets torn up.'

'So, OK, the rabbi stays behind and Mr Abelson leaves. What time was this?'

'Around half past eight.'

'And what happened then.'

'Mr Abelson turned into the alley that runs down the north side of the synagogue. His usual way home. It wasn't pitch black, but it was dark enough for the security lights around the synagogue to have switched on, which they do automatically at different times in the year. There's a high wall around the grounds of the synagogue on one side. with a gate at the far end which used to give access to the car-park. For security reasons it's a strong cast-iron gate with razor wire on top, and its only opened when the synagogue's being used.'

'So the gate was closed when Mr Abelson went down the alley.'

'Yes, but as he walked past it he saw through the bars someone moving around in what used to be the car-park. At first, he thought it must be the rabbi, and he called out to him. But then the figure moved into the light, and it turned out it certainly wasn't Rabbi Caton.'

'It was bright enough for him to be certain of that?'

'Oh, yes, he could be certain it wasn't the rabbi, because apparently the figure was wearing the robes of a medieval warrior monk.'

3

'A medieval warrior in full dress?' Fiona repeated the words.

'Yes,' Falcon replied. 'Apparently, he was wearing a white cape with a large black cross on his chest and something that looked very much like antlers on the top of his helmet. In his hand he held what the witness said was some kind of lance with a flag on the end, and he was dragging the Rabbi along the ground. Banging his head on the broken rubble.'

'So what did the witness do?' Fiona asked.

'He called out. He can't remember what he said, but the figure stopped and stood up straight. With only his eyes visible through slits in his helmet, and the antlers around his head, Mr Abelson said he looked like a vision from Hell.'

'And what did he do when Mr Abelson called out?'

'This is where I'm afraid Mr Abelson started to lose it, and his account becomes very confused. It appears that the attacker went through some kind of ritual sword fight before driving the lance into the rabbi's body. Then he carved something on the rabbi's chest with a dagger. But the details are vague, which is hardly suprprising since Mr Abelson was watching through the bars of the gate as his friend was butchered in front of him.'

'So how do you plan to direct this investigation?' Fiona asked.

'We'll use the force's modification of HOLMES, the Home Office Large Major Enquiry System. It will be carried out under a procedure designed to assess "Performance Management", which means it's continually under review. Everything transparent and up-front. Like working in a bloody goldfish bowl. Except this time, transparency may be no bad thing.'

'Why do you say that?' Fiona asked. 'My impression when we were working the Toy Breaker investigation was that transparency only bred stress.'

'True.' Mallory grinned at the reminder of his past. 'But this time, the circumstances may well merit transparency because of the ethnic connotations.'

'You mean the Jewish context?'

'That's exactly what I mean.'

'But surely the investigation doesn't require an officer of your exalted rank?'

'Upstairs thinks it does. There's a lot of nerves around at the moment because of the Faith Conference, and any misdemeanour with even a whiff of religion rings alarm bells.'

Fiona nodded. 'So what're the practical details of the investigation?'

'Major incident team with Gary as senior investigating officer, and DI Logan as number two. All the usual facilities. A first-class experienced team with every modern aid available to the police. We've got the best forensics, the best state-of-the-art data accessing and processing systems, the best expert IT advice. You want data on a particular criminal sub-set, we have access to all the Home Office and National Criminal Intelligence Service data bases.'

'Are you running the investigation with an executive team?'

'Yes, it's the only way to make effective tactical decisions.'

'And who's on it?'

'Me, DCI Falcon, DI Logan, DS Maltravers on data processing, and you, of course.'

'So what's the next step?'

'DI Logan's gone to pick up the leader of the synagogue council, Aaron Levi, and bring him here. Normally, we'd be happy to interview him at the synagogue itself, but this is a very sensitive issue and the media started gathering there at the first hint of an anti-Semitic incident. Naturally, Mr Levi wants to take care of his synagogue and the congregation. But he understands the problem and he's agreed to come to headquarters. Once he's here we can get a better idea of how to move the investigation forward, but first he insisted on going to the hospital to see Mr Abelson.'

'I agree, you need to speak to Mr Levi,' Fiona said. 'For one thing, he can provide background on the local Jewish community. And that could be very useful if this is an issue local to this particular synagogue. But. . . .' Her voice trailed off.

'But what?' Falcon asked.

'I can't help thinking that the set-up here is a bit elaborate. Dressing up in the robes of a warrior monk, for one thing. I don't think this is just another example of anti-Semitism. Who ever did this set out to deliberately kill the rabbi.'

'What are you saying?' Mallory didn't really want to ask the question.

'We might just have a fanatic out there with the single intent of killing Jews.'

4

'I sincerely hope you're wrong. Especially at this time.' Mallory spoke softly. Almost to himself.

But Falcon caught the words. 'At this time? You mean with the Faith Conference looming up?'

'Right. But let's hope that the timing's just a coincidence. That the murder of the Rabbi isn't connected to the conference. Now' – he turned to Fiona – 'while we wait for Mr Levi to arrive, do you have any first thoughts on the nature of the killing of the rabbi?'

'It's very early days yet, of course, but my immediate impression is that the whole thing reeks of symbolism. And very elaborate symbolism, at that. Which is intriguing. But on a practical level, a whole raft of questions jump straight to mind. First, why did the killer choose this particular synagogue, and this particular Rabbi? Is there anything special about either of them? But whatever the answers to those two questions, there's something strange here. As well as all the symbolism, like dressing as a warrior monk, the killing was almost ritualistic. In fact, as the witness described the way the killing was carried out, it definitely *was* ritualistic. Driving the lance into the victim's body, carving the sign into his flesh, it's almost sacrificial. And there are messages galore in there somewhere.'

'You think the killer is some kind of a religious nutter?' Mallory asked.

'A religious fanatic? Yes, like I said, I believe we could be dealing with a fanatic here. Perhaps even someone who thinks they are a messenger of God whose mission in life is to protect what they believe to be the "true faith". And don't forget, the warrior monks were Christians intent on freeing the Holy Land.'

'Wait a minute,' Falcon interrupted, 'isn't that a bit far fetched?'

'No, it's not. Especially when you consider the way the Rabbi's murder was staged. And, remember, anti-Semitism of this kind can happen on a mass scale. As it did in the Crusades and the Holocaust.'

'So what makes a religious fanatic?' Falcon asked.

'Ah, there lies a problem. Many factors can generate religious fervour, and—'

A that moment there was a knock on the door of the office and two men came in. One of them walked up to Mallory.

'This is Dr Levi, guv.' Most of Mallory's men still addressed him that way, even after his move upstairs.

'Thanks, Dan.' Mallory turned to the visitor, a tall, thin man dressed formally in a dark suit and wearing a black homburg.

'Dr Levi, thank you for agreeing to come here.' Mallory held out his hand. 'I know you must be wanted at the synagogue at this difficult time, but it's very important that we move forward quickly and I wanted to avoid media attention.'

Dr Levi shook Mallory's hand. 'I understand, Assistant Chief Constable, I would like to get back as soon as possible, but I fully realize there's a media circus around the synagogue at the moment. So, how can I help you?'

'Let me introduce my colleagues. You've already met Detective Inspector Logan who brought you here. This is Detective Chief Inspector Gary Falcon who will be heading the investigation into the Rabbi's murder, and this is Fiona Nightingale, a forensic psychiatrist who consults for the Garton police.'

Aaron Levi shook their hands. 'Dr Nightingale, I've heard of your work.'

'You're a psychiatrist?' Fiona asked, surprised that she hadn't heard of him since the psychiatric community in Garton was relatively small.

He smiled. 'No, I'm an orthopaedic surgeon, but my father was a child psychologist, and I keep up with the field. He always taught me that the mind is of great importance.'

'Of course.' Fiona nodded. 'Michael Levi. He worked with Holocaust survivors, didn't he?'

'Yes, he did.'

'Well, I'm sorry we have to meet under these circumstances.' Fiona said. 'But you'll understand why the police called me in to this investigation.'

'Yes. From what I understand from Phillip Abelson, the rabbi was killed under very strange circumstances.'

'You could say that,' said Falcon. 'Fiona thinks that the killer might have been carrying out some kind of ritual.'

'Yes, that was what Phillip said. A carefully organized assault, was the way he described the attack on the rabbi. And then, of course, there is the timing of the murder.'

'You mean with the Faith Conference coming up.' Mallory knew they would have to bring that out into the open at some stage.

'Yes, the Faith Conference. Are we looking for a connection here?' Dr Levi asked.

'We can't rule anything out at this stage,' Falcon said. 'Dr Levi, we know you haven't reported any anti-Semitic incidents at the synagogue lately because they would have been logged with our race relations unit. But has there been anything at all recently that might suggest anti-Jewish feelings?'

Aaron Levi sighed. 'There are always anti-Jewish feelings, Chief Inspector. But no, there's been no recent incidents in Garton as far as I am aware.'

'What form does the security at the synagogue take?' Mallory asked.

'All the walls are protected with razor wire, and there are CCTV cameras covering every inch of ground in the surrounding area. In addition, all visitors to the synagogue are subjected to security checks similar to those used at airports. And when there is a service on, we have patrols around the area. All the security has been overseen by the Community Security Trust, the Jewish security agency, and verified by the local police.'

Falcon started to say something, then stopped.

'You have a problem, Chief Inspector?'

'No, not really. It's just that the security seems a bit over the top.'

Aaron Levi nodded. 'I agree the security is very high on the James Street synagogue.'

'Why should that be?' Mallory asked.

'Because of its connection with the Guardians.'

5

'The Guardians?' Mallory asked. 'Who are they?'

'A Jewish sect chosen to safeguard a great treasure. A treasure they believe to be concealed somewhere inside the James Street synagogue.'

'What kind of treasure?'

'We're not sure. The legend has it that the *saphan*, which can translate as hidden treasure, was taken out of Israel by the members of a pharisaic sect at the time the Temple in Jerusalem fell, and was eventually brought to Europe where the sect settled in Prague. The treasure was kept there, guarded by members of the sect, who believed it was their sacred duty to keep it hidden.'

'And you don't know what this treasure is?' Fiona asked.

'No one outside the sect knows, although it's understood that it's some kind of artefact. But if I can return to the legend for a moment, it is believed that the nature of the treasure will only be revealed when the time is right, when it will do great good in the world.'

'How did the treasure get from Prague to Garton?' Fiona was finding herself intrigued by the legend.

'It was during the years of the Holocaust. The Jewish community of Prague, like many others in the lands overrun by the Nazis, was in great danger, particularly after the assassination of Reinhard Heydrich, so the elders of the sect decided to move the treasure. It was spirited out of Prague under the noses of the SS, and the idea was to take it to a place of safety in the United States via a route that had been used before to transport religious items out of Europe. The Prague Treasure was brought here to Garton by two members of the sect for eventual transhipment across the Atlantic to New York. Until that could be done, it was hidden somewhere in the James Street synagogue. But the place where the two members of the sect were staying was destroyed in a bombing raid and both men were killed. The location of the treasure has remained a secret ever since.'

'And you've no idea what this treasure may be.'

'No, but the sect still survives. After the end of World War Two, the remaining members of the sect who'd escaped the Nazis emigrated to the United States and formed a small orthodox community in the north of New York State. They still believe that the treasure is hidden somewhere in the James Street synagogue here in Garton.'

'But surely members of the sect have looked for the treasure?' Falcon asked.

'Oh, yes, they have.' For a moment there was the suggestion of a twinkle in Aaron Levi's eyes. 'In fact, the synagogue has done quite well out of the legend of the treasure; it flourishes as a tourist centre on the back of it. But, no, the treasure has not been found yet. Although the synagogue does have strong links with the sect in the US.'

'You think the death of the Rabbi could be connected to the treasure,' Mallory asked.

'Perhaps.' Aaron Levi sounded tired suddenly. 'Now, if you'll excuse me I'll get back to the synagogue. You have my mobile number if you need to contact me.'

'We do, and thank you again for coming in. I'll arrange a car to take you back.' Mallory ushered him out of the office.

'Ritual killings, ancient legends, hidden artefacts and secret sects.' Falcon muttered. 'It's like something out of an *Indiana Jones* movie.'

6

When Mallory came back he looked at Fiona and Falcon. 'Before we break up, let's see where we are.'

He led them outside the office onto the platform, and stopped in front of a glass screen. Then he picked up a red marker pen from the shelf under it and began to write a series of headings on the glass. As each category was identified, Mallory summarized the key facts.

1 - The murder.

'It took place at the James Street synagogue and the man murdered was a Rabbi well known in the local Jewish community. It was a particularly vicious, and according to Fiona, possibly ritualistic, killing.'

2 - The Killer.

'He was dressed as a medieval warrior monk and may be a religious fanatic with anti-Semitic leanings. Anything else to add at this stage, Fiona?'

'Like I said, early days yet. But a couple of things stand out. On the one hand, the actual murder was violent. In fact, driving in the lance like that showed a very *high degree* of violence. But, on the other hand, the scene itself was carefully arranged. Which means the killer was in control, and what's more, he wasn't fazed by having the witness watching him through the railings. Brutal violence and icy control. A heady mixture.'

'So, how do we proceed?' Mallory moved to the screen again and wrote a third heading.

3 - Requirements.

'OK.' Falcon took over now. 'The crime scene has been secured and we'll get a full briefing from the SOCOs tomorrow. We have excellent CCTV coverage of the incident from the synagogue security, and that's already being studied in fine detail. We also have a major piece of evidence; the lance that was left behind at the scene. So far, all I can tell you is that it carried a dragon pennant on the tip.'

'A dragon pennant.' Fiona drummed her fingers against the side of the glass screen. 'Does that have religious connotations, I wonder? Is the dragon symbolic?'

'We'll have to look into that,' Falcon said. 'But at the moment, we need to concentrate on building up all the background information we can. Every member of the synagogue congregation will have to be interviewed, and we'll have to delve into the rabbi's background. Aaron Levi can be our point of contact there.'

'What about the sect in America?' Fiona asked.

'For the moment we keep them in reserve. If it turns out that we do need anything more on them, we go to Aaron Levi again. We also have to contact all other religious leaders in the community to find out if there has been even a suggestion of anything anti-Semitic to emerge over the past few months. In addition, we have to trawl the internet, particularly the chat rooms, to see if we can pick up any growing anti-Semitic activity there. Sergeant Maltravers's team can handle that. Any other angles to cover at this stage? Fiona?'

'I suggest we access national resources and build up our own data base on known religious fanatics, and look for possible suspects that way.'

Mallory nodded. 'Sergeant Maltravers can take care of that as well. Anything else?'

'The outfit the killer was wearing,' Fiona said. 'We need to bring in an expert to look at it. Someone who can comment on its authenticity. Maybe even be able to suggest why the killer dressed in this particular way. And I suggest Professor Brinton from the university. His field is the Crusades, and he's an authority on warrior monks, or monks of war as they're sometimes called.'

'Good, can you talk to him?'

'Yes, I'll do that. I'll go and see him at the university.'

'Anything else?'

'Yes, I'd like to look at the CCTV footage of the killing.'

'No problem. The original disc is with the techies, but we had a copy made.'

He walked over to a numbered cardboard box against the far wall of the dais and came back with a disc which he inserted into the play tray of a DVD connected to one of the plasma TV sets. For the next few minutes they watched the murder unfold.

When the killer first appeared on the screen he was dragging the unconscious body of the rabbi behind him with one hand, the other carrying the lance with the dragon banner on it. He arranged the body against a pile of rubble. Then he placed the lance on the ground and drew a broadsword from a scabbard on his waist. At that stage he began what looked like an imaginary sword fight, wielding his weapon in a series of arcs. Then he threw it to the ground and picked up the lance which he suddenly drove through the victim's chest. After that he withdrew the lance and planted it in the ground. For a moment, he looked at the body, before pulling back the victim's clothing and carving something onto his chest with a dagger which he took from his belt. When he was finished he picked up the sword and walked away.

'Thank you.' Fiona nodded to Falcon. 'From the way the figure moved, I'd say it was a man, but I think I'll keep my comments on the way he staged the killing till later.'

Falcon seemed happy with that. 'So, is that it for now?'

'Except for one more thing.' Mallory sighed.

'Which is?' Fiona asked.

'The Faith Conference. I sincerely hope I'm wrong, but if the murder at the synagogue is in any way connected to the conference then believe me, the brown stuff will hit the fan. Big time.'

'I've heard about the conference, of course.' Fiona said. 'But can you fill me in with the details?'

Mallory had called the briefing for 7.30 the next morning.

'DI Logan's been running security for the conference on the team headed up by Superintendent Casterly. So I'm appointing Dan as liaison officer between the murder investigation and the conference team. Can you brief us on the Faith Conference, Dan?'

DI Logan smiled at Fiona. They'd worked together on the Anger Man investigation, and she knew something of his history in the Garton Force. Apparently, he'd joined at the same time as DCI Falcon and from the first day Logan had seemed to resent the fast track university graduate. Although he appeared to be a promising detective, Logan soon acquired the reputation of a troublemaker with no respect for rank, and his career had languished in the doldrums, until Mallory recognized his genius for data processing technology, and moved him in to head up a joint Garton Police/Home Office anti-terrorist pilot programme. On the back of that, Logan had been made Casterly's deputy in the team which ran security for the Faith Conference.

So in many ways, Fiona thought, Logan was an up and coming man now, and on a personal front, although the two weren't exactly drinking buddies, a kind of truce had developed between him and Falcon.

'OK,' Logan nodded. 'The conference. It's an international gathering with the formal title "Three Faiths – One God", and the purpose is to address the question to what extent do the three major religions, Islam, Judaism and Christianity, believe in the same God. It's one of the most important multi-faith gatherings held for years, and there's real hope that it will bring the three religions closer together. Maybe even spawn peace initiatives.'

'But surely,' Fiona persisted, 'fanatics and hardliners on all sides will be against that?'

'They may well be. But the conference is no more than an exploration of communality in the way the religions perceive God.'

Fiona gaped at him, and Logan grinned. 'OK, I've been living with this for months now and I guess I've picked up the jargon. But the conference is important. So much so that it's to be opened by the Secretary General of the United Nations, no less. So it was a great honour for Garton to be chosen as the host city.'

'Why was Garton chosen?' Fiona asked.

'For one thing, it's a port with strong Jewish and Muslim communities, as well as Catholic and Protestant Christian populations. So it has a strong multi-cultural background. Garton is also iconic because it has two cathedrals on the same street. One

Anglican, one Catholic.'

'And the security, is it a nightmare? With the international dimension, I mean?' Fiona asked.

Logan grinned. 'I've had easier jobs. Delegates are coming from all over the world, and I suppose I'll have a few more grey hairs when it's all over.'

'What are the chances of the rabbi's murder being linked to the Faith Conference?' Mallory asked.

Dan Logan shrugged. 'We've not picked up any intel that suggests an anti-Semitic connection. Not even a faint whisper.'

Mallory sounded relieved. 'So let's hope it stays that way. Because if this killing, dreadful as it is, can be contained to a single act of anti-Semitism, we won't have the complication of the Faith Conference hanging over our every action.'

But within a few hours that hope was shattered.

7

The garden was small, laid out in a very formal design. On three sides it was protected by tall hedges, the only access being a small arch in the hedge facing the road, and on the fourth side it was overlooked by the wall of a mosque. In the garden itself, four squares of lawn were enclosed by box hedges, and in the centre there was a fountain with seats arranged around it. A haven of peace in the city sprawl.

Except that now, it was far from a peaceful haven.

When Fiona and Falcon got there the gates had been secured by police scenes-of-crime tape, and in the centre of one of the squares of lawn a plastic tent had been erected. The officer on the gate opened it for Fiona and Falcon and a SOCO came over and issued them with protective clothing from a large plastic bag. As they put on the garments, Falcon smiled grimly. 'Getting to be a habit, this dressing up.'

'So what happened here?' Fiona asked the SOCO.

'Same MO as the death of the rabbi. A dragon banner driven through the body, then stuck in the ground. Just one difference though.'

'And what's that?' Fiona thought Falcon sounded strained as he asked the question.

'The victim isn't Jewish. He's an important leader in the Muslim community.'

'Was anything carved into his flesh?' Fiona asked.

'Yes, a crescent,' the SOCO replied.

'It would seem our killer's spreading his wings,' Falcon turned to Fiona. 'So what do you want to do?' he asked, as they stopped outside the tent.

'Did the CCTV pick up anything?'

'Yes, the cameras caught the entire episode.'

'OK, so for now I'd just like to get a feel for the scene. That's all at this stage. Then I'd like to see the CCTV coverage.'

'First impressions?' Falcon asked Fiona, when they were back in the major incident room.

'In some ways this murder was a carbon copy of the first. Both were acts of extreme violence carried out in a public space and the murders appear to have been executed in the same way. And both scenes were carefully staged.'

'But there were differences between the two crimes.' Falcon started to count off on his fingers. 'One, in each case the killer was dressed as a medieval warrior monk, but from the CCTV at the two sites it seems that the outfits were different. Maybe your professor at the university can throw some light on that.'

'I'll get onto him as soon as I can,' Fiona replied.

'Two,' Falcon carried on counting, 'the signs carved into the victim's bodies were different. The Star of David, and the Crescent. Three, the most important difference of all, of course: the first victim was Jewish and the second was Muslim. And both were important leaders in their communities. So we can be certain that there was nothing random about these two killings.'

'Most certainly not. Too many similarities. And I think we can rule out a copycat murder because too many details were the same. Details that wouldn't necessarily be known to a second killer. No, these two victims were carefully selected, and killed by the same person.'

'It does look that way,' Falcon agreed.

'So what have we got? A violent killer who selects his victims and remains in control of the situation to the extent that he arranges the crime scene. But this time the killer switched victims and killed a Muslim. So we can rule out an anti-Semitic motive.'

'But not a religious motive?'

'Oh, no, we certainly can't rule that out. Look at the evidence.

The killer dresses as a warrior monk. A different order of monk in each crime, but, nonetheless, a monk. A religious soldier. The symbolism's all too apparent. And then we have what is perhaps the most important pointer so far to the killer's motive. The two victims were important religious, not secular, leaders in their respective communities. So in carrying out these murders, the killer is making a statement. He's sending a message that leaves absolutely no doubt that he's picking off religious figureheads.'

'ACC Mallory's worst nightmare. A religious killer on the streets with the Faith Conference looming. Question is, is our killer against *all* faiths?'

'And that could be perhaps the most important question of all. Is the killer on a crusade against those he sees as the enemies of Christ, to preserve the forces of *light*? Or is he on a mission to destroy all faiths and promote the forces of *darkness*? In other words, the Devil?'

8

When Mallory came in he was accompanied by a tall, thin man with a neatly trimmed beard. He was dressed in a sober business suit.

'This is Dr Sharif, President of the Garton Muslim Council.' When he'd made the introductions, Mallory led the way to the long table on the dais and they sat down.

'Firstly, I'd like to offer my condolences to Dr Sharif for the loss of the imam.'

'Thank you.' Dr Sharif inclined his head in acknowledgement. 'He was a good man, and will be greatly missed.'

'Can you think of any reason why anyone would want to kill him?' Mallory asked.

'There are always, how shall I phrase it, hotheads in the community. And I mean the wider community, not just the Muslims. But in this case, I really cannot think that the imam would have been targeted for his views.'

'What was his attitude to the present state of affairs with respect to Muslims in the UK?'

Dr Sharif smiled. A sad smile. 'I think we are fencing, Assistant Chief Constable. A sign of the times, I fear. What you are really asking, is what was the imam's stance on terrorism? But political correctness forbids you to ask directly. Am I right?'

Mallory nodded, accepting Dr Sharif's point. 'Unfortunately, that's true. Walking on eggshells doesn't even come close to it. But I would like to know where the imam stood on the role of Muslims in the wider community. It might well relate to why he was killed.'

'If we were to put a label on him, it would be that of a moderate. He passionately believed that Muslims should integrate into what you called the 'wider community'. But he did not advocate diluting our religion. In his eyes, the teachings of the Koran were absolute, but he fully recognized that we live in the UK, and must abide by the law of the UK. Perhaps that upset some of the fanatics, but I do not think he would have been killed for his views. Like Rabbi Caton, the imam was a respected moderate.'

'Did the two men know each other?' Fiona asked.

Dr Sharif thought for a moment. 'They may have met at various functions from time to time, but as far as I am aware, they did not know each other well. You were looking for a connection between them?'

Fiona nodded. 'Yes, something that could explain why those two men were selected by the killer.'

'I'm sorry, but I do not think there is any connection of that nature between them.'

'So we're back to the fact that they were both leaders in their respective communities. Would you say that the imam was the senior leader of the Muslims in Garton?' Falcon asked.

'No, but the spiritual leader is too old and frail to play an active role in the community. That was why the imam was selected to give one of the keynote speeches at the forthcoming Faith Conference.'

'He was to give a keynote speech?' Falcon repeated the words as a question.

'Yes, it was one of three, to be given at the opening session. Delivered on behalf of the Muslim, the Jewish and the Christian faiths.'

'Shit.' Mallory didn't even begin to apologize for his language as he turned to DI Logan. 'Dan, do you have a number if you need to contact the conference organizers on security matters?'

'Yes, I have a direct line to the conference office.'

'Get onto them now. Find out who's down to deliver the other two keynote speeches.'

Dan Logan walked to the end of the platform and dialled a number on his mobile. When he came back he spoke directly to Mallory.

'Not good news, guv. The Jewish speech was to be given by Rabbi Caton.'

'So there is a connection between them. The Faith Conference. It looks as if someone really is out to sabotage it.'

'And that's not the main problem at the moment.' Falcon snapped his fingers. 'Dr Sharif said there were to be three keynote speakers. Who's giving the speech for the Christian faith?'

'Archbishop Conron.' Dan Logan replied.

'So we have to get to him before the killer does. Let me find where he is and put him under protective cover before we lose the third keynote speaker. I'll get in touch with the cathedral office and locate him. But I need the number.'

He stood up from the table and walked back down the platform. He spoke to one of the officers sitting at the row of computers, and waited until he brought the cathedral website on the screen. Falcon read the contact number and dialled it on the phone by the side of the computer. It took several transfers before he reached the archbishop's office, and when he finally got through he was sidetracked to an official. After a few moments he came back to the table.

'It would appear that the archbishop is in retreat. To prepare himself for the conference apparently.'

'Then we'd better get a security net around him soonest.' Mallory sounded worried. 'Because if we don't, he's a dead man walking.'

9

Dan Logan went off to arrange the security around the archbishop, and Dr Sharif left to attend to a number of matters at the Muslim Council.

When they'd gone, Mallory sent out for coffee, then turned to Fiona. 'We learned one very important piece of evidence from Dr Sharif. The two men who have been killed are not just religious leaders in the community: they were both down to give keynote speeches at the Faith Conference. Any thoughts on that?'

'Well, there can be no doubt now that both killings had a strong religious motive. Agreed?'

Mallory nodded, content to let Fiona lead.

'The important question is where's the killer coming from? When he performs the murders, and I use the word *perform* deliberately, he dresses as a warrior monk from the days of the Crusades. Very definitely a Christian figure. So is this a crusade against what the killer sees as the enemies of Christ?'

'Is there anything you can give us that might indicate the kind of man we're dealing with here?' Falcon asked. 'The God Slayer as the media have started calling him.'

'Dramatic, but understandable,' Fiona replied. 'Let's move over to a whiteboard and see what we can put together.'

Mallory and Falcon followed Fiona as she walked to the back of the platform. Two whiteboards were already in use; one dedicated to the rabbi, and the other to the imam. Both had photos of the victims and the scene of the crime.

Fiona moved to the third whiteboard in the line and picked up a black marker pen. Then she started talking, writing comments on the board as she did so.

'In both cases the killer wore a helmet, so we couldn't see his face. But similarities in the MOs indicate that we're dealing with a single killer. Probably a man because of the strength required to handle the broadsword and drive the banner into the victims' bodies. Because the two victims were religious leaders in their communities, we can assume a religious dimension in both killings. And I think there's something else here. The two murders were violent, very violent when the lance was driven into the victim's chest. But all the time the killer was in complete control. We know that because he carefully arranged the crime scenes.'

'And that's important?' Mallory asked.

'Yes, I think it is. Because it gives us our first real insight into the killer's mind.'

'How?'

'Because it begs the question, why employ such violence? Was it an act of revenge? Even if it wasn't, it's highly unlikely that anyone would display that degree of violence if they didn't have a personal reason to do so. Perhaps someone who has turned against their faith for some reason. Maybe they hold a grudge against religion. Possibly because of some traumatic trigger event. We don't have enough evidence to confirm that yet. But I think we can tentatively identify our killer as a man with strong religious beliefs whose faith has been challenged and, it would seem, found wanting. That's the only way to account for this level of violence.'

Fiona stepped back to the board. 'So what have we got so far?' She began to write on the surface.

1 A single killer for both murders:
2 Both murders have a strong religious dimension – one of a rabbi, one of an imam.
3 The killer has a violent streak, but he remains very much in control and carefully arranges the crime scene.
4 The degree of violence may well indicate anger, or revenge perhaps.
5 The killer was probably a deeply religious man who's been forced to question his beliefs. Maybe because of a trauma of some kind.

'So how can we use this preliminary profile?' Falcon, came in straight away with a policeman's question.

Fiona thought for a moment. 'Let's follow up first on the assumption that the killer has been a religious person whose beliefs have been challenged by some trigger event. We need to liase with all the churches, synagogues and mosques in Garton and the surrounding area. See if they can turn up anyone who fits that profile. We can start off with an e-mail sweep. Get the addresses from the central administrators and e-mail each individual church, synagogue and mosque. Most will have an e-mail contact in this day and age, I'm sure. And in any case we can identify those that don't and reach them another way. But the sweep's worth a try.'

'Sergeant Maltravers is running data handling. She's at another meeting at the moment, but I'll get her started on the search soonest,' Falcon said.

'Ask her to concentrate on the Christian churches to begin with.'

'Why?'

'Because the killer dressed up as a warrior monk. We don't know why yet, but the monks were Christians. So we might as well use that as a starting point.'

'Anything else at this stage?' Mallory was pushing, but Fiona knew the kind of pressure this investigation would generate. And it was Falcon who answered.

'Yes, Fiona has a contact at the university, and I'd like to go with her when she talks to him about the warrior monk costumes the killer wears.'

'Good idea,' Mallory agreed.

At that moment Dan Logan came onto the dais, and he looked worried.

'Bad news. I contacted the place where the archbishop's in retreat, and it seems he's gone missing.'

10

The line of police officers with the dogs moved slowly across the sweep of grass towards the wooded high ground. Dan Logan followed behind.

The retreat was in the countryside outside Garton, an Elizabethan manor house that had been used by the Anglican Church as a place of retreat and peace for many years. Archbishop Mountleroy had arrived two days before to finalize his keynote speech to the Faith Conference away from the distractions of running the archdiocese.

That morning he'd left the house alone, saying that he wanted to walk the gardens where he could think in peace. But no one had seen him since and the party sent out to find him following the message from DI Logan had drawn a blank.

The police line reached the trees and moved inside. It was darker there as the branches cut out much of the light, forming dappled patches of shade. The ground was uneven, with occasional outcrops of limestone, and the police struggled to keep the line as they advanced. Then one of the dogs barked, the sound carrying on the crisp spring air.

'Over here,' the dog handler called out and Logan hurried forward.

He stopped on the edge of a steep depression in the ground that was almost filled in with jumbled blocks of limestone. The dog was pulling on his lead as he tried to get down, but his handler held him back.

'Down there,' the handler called out as Logan approached. 'There's something caught between two rocks.'

Logan looked at the ground and saw it had been scuffed up around the edge of the depression. Then he went down the slope, almost slipping on the steep surface. At the base of the depression he paused and looked through the gap formed between two large slabs of rock which had jammed against each other. On the far side a body had been wedged against the stone, a dragon banner lying on the ground beside it. Logan bent forward and examined the body. The chest had been exposed and a cross had been carved into the flesh.

'Pity we didn't contact him sooner, and we'll sure as hell take flak for that.'

Mallory had called a meeting of the executive team as soon as DI Logan returned to HQ.

'But for the moment, let's move on. Dan left as soon as the SOCO team arrived but he took a number of photographs of the crime scene for Fiona to look at. I thought that might waste less time than going out there, but, of course, we can take you to the scene if need be.'

'I don't think it will be necessary to visit this particular crime scene,' Fiona replied. 'We'll get the full details from the scenes-of-crime report, but as far as I can tell this murder has the essential features of the first two killings. The exception is that this time the body was hidden, which was why the people from the retreat didn't find it when they searched. But we don't know why the body was hidden.'

'I think I can answer that,' Dan Logan interrupted. 'The ground was disturbed around the edge of the depression. I think it shows up on one of the pics. Yes, there.' He pointed to one of the glossy prints. 'I think there was a struggle, and that one, or both, of the men fell down the side and were caught between the rocks. At that stage, the archbishop must still have been alive, because there was no blood on the disturbed ground. But there were copious amounts of it pooled at the base of the crack and scattered on the walls. I don't think the body was so much hidden deliberately, more that it fell into the crack and wedged there. But the interesting point was that as well as the lance, the uniform worn by the killer was left at the scene this time.'

'Now why was that, I wonder?' Mallory muttered the question.

'Symbolism,' Fiona said. 'He wanted us to know who he was representing. Just as he did in the first two murders. But there was no CCTV to record the killing this time. So he deliberately left the evidence behind.'

'Do we know which uniform it was?' Falcon asked.

'No,' Fiona answered. 'But Dan took a photograph of it, and I can show it to Professor Brinton when I go to see him.'

'Anything else?' Mallory asked.

'Yes, when I phoned Professor Brinton to make an appointment to see him, I asked about the dragon banners that were left behind at all three crime scenes.'

'Go on.'

'Apparently, dragons have featured in legends from all over the world. But the most important aspect of the mythology from our point of view is that dragons were often used as a symbol of the Devil. And don't forget, the dragon banners weren't just left behind, the lances they were attached to were the actual murder weapons.'

'And what's the significance of that?'

'Before I try to answer, can I look at the CCTV coverage of both of the first two murders? I've already seen them, but I'd like another look.'

'Sure.' Falcon walked over and selected two discs from one of the numbered cardboard boxes stacked on shelves on the far side of the dais, and for the next few minutes they watched the CCTV footage of the two murders.

'There, pause it a moment.' Fiona indicated a sequence shot at the rear of the synagogue. 'To begin with the killer got the victim positioned the way he wanted, with the dragon banner close by. Once he's set the scene, two things happen. First, he raises the broadsword. But look carefully. The movements are as if he's fighting against an unseen assailant. It's a ritual. Then he throws the sword down and drives the dragon banner into the victim's chest.

That's the stage at which the actual killing took place, with the dragon banner. Can we see the footage of the second murder, please?'

Falcon changed the discs, and ran the sequence in the garden by the mosque. The details were the same as those at the synagogue.

'So, where does this get us?' Mallory sounded puzzled.

'I don't want to sound too upbeat, but I think it gives us another insight into the killer's mind. It's been there since the first murder, but as I said, we didn't pick up the significance. In setting up these macabre murders, we assumed that we were meant to believe that by some twisted logic the killer in the ritual was a warrior monk. But we've been wrong. The monks were there as *defenders* of the faith. That was the whole point of the pretend fight using the broadsword. It's all been a show. Pure theatre. But theatre with a message.'

'What message?' Mallory asked.

'All the warrior monk orders were devoted to preserving the true faith. Or, rather, what they saw as the true faith, and at first, like everybody else, I assumed the God Slayer had simply turned the mirror round. That he'd used the warrior monks as an instrument to destroy, rather than preserve, the true faith.'

'But now?'

'Now it seems that the warrior monks were there as symbols to preserve the faith. And they all failed. All of the orders. Because the single force behind all three killings is the dragon. The Devil. Look.'

She walked over to the whiteboard she'd used earlier. 'The last point, number five, highlighted the fact that the killer was a deeply religious man who'd been forced to question his faith. Well, now we can go a step further and start to get into his mind: what the killer is telling us is that he's renounced all recognized religion. Christian, Jewish and Muslim. He staged the killings so that the Devil prevailed. That's what I meant about giving us an insight into his mind. I think he's suffered some kind of religious trauma that has tipped him over the edge.'

'But why go to all the trouble of setting-up the complicated ritual to show he's rejected all religion?'

'Because he's playing mind games with us. Staging the murders like a theatrical director would. A very sick theatrical director.'

11

As Fiona walked along the cloistered passage with Falcon she marvelled, not for the first time, at how the old university buildings seemed so remote from the rest of the city. As if they were somehow suspended in time.

Professor Brinton's office was at the end of a corridor where the stone walls were hung with heavily framed portraits of stern-faced gentlemen wearing a variety of academic robes. When she knocked on the door it was opened by a middle-aged man dressed in a loud check sports coat and corduroys, with a bright yellow shirt and blue patterned cravat. The caricature of a typical academic, Fiona thought.

'Doctor Nightingale. And Detective Chief Inspector Falcon.' He held out his hand. 'Come in, please.' His voice was rich and vibrant; a voice used to holding classes of students in thrall.

They shook hands and Fiona looked around the office. It was a shrine to scholarship, with bookshelves stacked haphazardly with leather bound volumes, journals and green-backed Ph.D. theses. There were glass cases against two of the walls, filled with a variety of artefacts which included old battle pennants, weapons and documents. The only apparent pandering to modern times was a high-powered computer on a small plastic desk, with discs and instruction manuals on shelves at the side.

Professor Brinton lead Fiona and Falcon to a coffee table under a lead latticed window that looked down on the central quadrangle of the university complex. When they were seated, the professor rummaged in a pocket of his jacket and extracted a large curved meerschaum pipe, then held up his hand quickly. 'It's all right, I know the rules. The university is a non-smoking environment. Damn PC nonsense, of course, but there you are. And rest assured, I don't light it.'

Falcon grinned. 'Well, I can see how it protects people from the effects of passive smoking, but a blanket ban does seem a little draconian.'

'Anyway, it's a done deed.' The professor sighed. 'So, how can I help you? I must say I was intrigued by your call. How you wanted to speak to me about a subject you couldn't talk about over the phone.'

'Sorry about that,' Fiona said. 'It was a bit over the top, I suppose, but the matter is very serious. I'm a forensic psychiatrist. I work at the Waring Special Hospital and I also run a short course at the university in offender profiling. And we're here because we need your help in a murder investigation.'

'Now I really am intrigued.'

Fiona hesitated for a moment. 'Look, some of what I'm going to tell you isn't in the public domain yet, and I'd like to ask if you would treat anything I say in confidence. At least until it's released to the media.'

'Agreed,' The professor nodded. 'So, am I right in guessing that this has to do with the murders of the three religious leaders?'

When Fiona looked surprised, he grinned. 'You're right, the police haven't released much. But the media have gone overboard on the murders. They've already tagged the perpetrator the God Slayer. It's no quantum leap of the imagination to assume your visit is connected to the killings. So, how can I help?'

'Thank you.' Fiona opened the briefcase she'd brought with her and took out two A4-sized glossy black and white prints which she spread out on the table top.

'These are stills taken from CCTV coverage of the two murders. What we're interested in is the warrior monk uniforms worn by the men in these pictures. This one' – she tapped one of the prints with her finger – 'was worn when the rabbi was killed.'

The professor picked up the print and studied it for a moment. 'Warrior monk, indeed. This is the habit of the Grand Master of the

Teutonic Knights circa 1300. And you say it was worn by the man who killed the rabbi.'

'Yes. So what was special about these Teutonic Knights?'

The professor fingered his pipe as he considered his answer. 'What do you know about warrior monks, the so-called "Monks of War"?'

'Very little really.' Fiona answered for both of them.

'So, let me just fill in some background. There were three major orders of warrior monks. The Knights Templar, the Teutonic Knights, and the Hospitallers, or Knights of Malta. They were literally monks with swords. Noblemen who took on vows of obedience, chastity and poverty, just as ordinary monks did. But they also had a fighting role. They provided the church with soldiers for the Crusades, and that is perhaps what they are most famous for. But the Teutonic Knights especially also fought in Holy Wars in northern Europe.'

'Would you say the members of these orders were fanatics?' Falcon asked.

'To a point, yes, I suppose you could call them fanatics. At the time of the Crusades there was a great deal of fanaticism about, especially after the Vatican called for the Holy Land to be liberated.'

'Who did they consider their enemies?' Falcon came in again.

'Ah, I can see where you're coming from. A man wearing the uniform of a Teutonic Knight kills the rabbi of a synagogue. So was this an anti-Semitic act?'

'Was it?' Falcon pushed the question.

The professor shrugged. 'As I said, the main battles in the Crusades were fought against the Muslims to liberate the Holy Lands, but there were also Crusades in Europe. For example, against the Slavs, the Cathars and, yes, the Jews.'

'And this one?' Fiona tapped the other print.

The professor placed the first print down and looked at the second one. 'The Grand Master of the Knights Templar, around the same time as the other fellow.'

'One more.' Fiona took the photograph taken by Dan Logan from her briefcase and passed it to the professor. 'This uniform was left at the scene where the archbishop was killed.'

The professor took the print and examined it carefully. 'This is the robe of the Grand Master of the Hospitallers, or Knight of Malta. So you've got a full set now. One each for the three major orders of warrior monks.'

'Is there any reason why the killer should dress in different uniforms to kill a Jew, a Muslim and a Christian?'

'None that jumps to mind, no.'

'So why use the warrior monks at all?'

The professor smiled. 'To answer that, one would have to get inside the mind of the killer and I thought that was your job.'

Fiona grinned, acknowledging the point. 'You're right, of course.'

'But there is one strange thing, though,' The professor said.

'And what's that?'

'These are not just common or garden uniforms. These are the robes of the grand masters of the three orders.'

'You think that's significant?' Fiona asked.

'I don't know. But if the idea is to project an image, then you might as well go to the top. The figureheads.'

'What do you mean, project an image?'

'Maybe the killer is staging a show.'

Fiona remembered what she'd said to Mallory and Falcon earlier. That the killer was staging the murders like a theatrical director would. But for the moment she left it at that.

'Just one more question, Professor. A purely practical one this time. Do the uniforms the killer was wearing look authentic to you, or are they just rough copies?'

The professor examined the prints again, taking more care this time. 'As far as I can tell, they all look authentic enough.'

'So someone has gone to the trouble of recreating medieval warrior monks' uniforms.' Fiona was thinking aloud. 'Of course, it's possible they were obtained from a theatrical costumers. The police team are already checking that out. But we'll have to leave it for the moment.' She stood up. 'Thank you for giving us your time, Professor.'

As they walked back through the cloisters Fiona mulled over how what they'd learned from the professor fitted into the bigger picture.

47

Three keynote speakers at the Faith Conference, three orders of warrior monk. The killer had been dressed in the uniforms of the grand masters of the three major warrior monk orders: the Teutonic Knights, the Knights Templar and the Hospitallers.

But why were the murders so carefully staged? Was it just because the killer was playing mind games with them? Or was there some other reason?

12

Mallory met the Deputy Chief Constable in a pub by the river on the outskirts of Garton.

It was a favourite place for their meetings, and they sat at a table by the window overlooking the wild sweep of marshland that ran down towards the river. Mallory remembered the view the last time they'd met here. But it had been deep in winter then, under a wild darkening sky. Now, spring had softened the harsh countryside with patches of wild flowers fringing the edges of the creeks.

But the man sitting opposite Mallory seemed somehow to have dragged a reminder of that bleak winter with him, letting it occupy the space between them. Then, just for a moment, the bleakness in his expression lifted as he raised his glass.

'Congratulations on your forthcoming nuptials, David. I hope you'll both be very happy. But a vicar?' The DCC grinned mischievously. 'You sure you're ready for that? I mean, a vicar. Won't she try and reform you, poor girl?'

Mallory smiled back, well used by now to the banter from his fellow officers. 'She might have a job on her hands, I agree. But for some reason I don't understand, she seems to think it might just be worth it. You'll be receiving your invite to the wedding soon, by the way.'

'Thanks, Mary will be pleased. But to turn to more serious matters. Bad business this God Slayer affair. Particularly at this time.'

'You mean with the conference coming up?'

'Partly that, yes.' He broke off to sip his pint, and when he spoke again the bleakness was back in his eyes. 'You know it's almost ten years now since the Garton Force underwent a major reorganization?'

'Yes, I know that, and you were the officer who drove it. In fact, it was part of your brief when you were appointed.'

'That's right, and now there's every chance there's about to be another reorganization. But this time I certainly won't be driving it.'

'I've not got wind of anything big in the air.' Mallory sounded surprised.

'At the moment it's only got to the stage of defining boundaries.' The DCC finished his beer and put the glass down on the table. 'Let me get some more drinks.'

He walked over to the bar, and when he came back he was carrying two pint glasses. 'I've ordered a couple of steak sandwiches. They'll help mop up the beer.' He sat down and passed one of the glasses to Mallory.

'Cheers.' Mallory raised his pint. 'Now, what was the expression you used? *Defining boundaries*?'

'That's right, and at the heart of it is a position paper written by the chief constable.'

'You mean he wrote it on his own?'

'Oh, no, not on his own. It was drawn up after informal discussions with a big hitter from the mayor's office, and two very ambitious new members of the Police Authority. And it's a very confidential document.'

'But surely, the chief constable wouldn't make policy changes without sounding out the top brass on the force first?'

'Oh, he would, and there's nothing wrong with that at all. He'd say he was taking civilian views before turning to the force.'

'And the secrecy?'

'Nothing unusual there either. He'd point out that he didn't want the exercise leaked yet because it might well come to nothing.'

'OK, but why is the chief constable thinking of reorganization now?'

'Two main triggers. The first is the forthcoming retirement of the Assistant Chief Constable, George Clarke. The chief constable wants to take the opportunity of appointing a reformer to the post.

Someone from outside the Garton Force.'

'Do we know who?'

'Paul Minter's name's been banded about.'

'Not the one who brought all that grief to the Met with the changes he made to middle management?'

'None other.'

'Bloody hell, that'll rattle a few cages.'

A waitress came over then with the steak sandwiches and a bowl of chips, and for the next few minutes the two men ate in silence.

'Um, very good.' Mallory wiped his hands on a paper napkin. 'You said there were two triggers. What was the other one?'

'The Flanagan Report. It recommends some very far reaching reforms of the police, particularly as regards improving performance, increasing support policing, better resource management, less bureaucracy and the involvement of local people in neighbourhood policing. Reforms that will eventually have to be implemented across the board, and the chief constable thinks there may be initiative money available for those forces that move first. Particularly in the integration of the police, national and local government in mainstream policing, which is a pet theme of his.'

Mallory raised his eyebrows, and the DCC grinned. 'All right, so I can trot out all the jargon like the next man. Good God, I should be able to, the time I've spent reading all the crap that comes down from the Home Office.'

'Have you seen a copy of the position paper?' Mallory asked.

For a moment the DCC didn't reply. 'Believe it or not, but I was once considered to be a reformer myself. Now alas, I fear I'm not flavour of the month with our leader. Oh, we work together well enough on a day-to-day basis. And in time, no doubt I'll be drawn into the loop over any changes, but as far as the chief constable's concerned I'm afraid I'm definitely no longer the future. But I still have a few friends in high places, inside and outside the force. People I've worked closely with for years. And to answer your question, yes, I have seen a copy of the position paper.'

'And?' Mallory was beginning to think the DCC was being so circumspect that it was like teasing information from a suspect being interviewed under caution.

'In a way, the paper's quite innovative. And if it's implemented it'll bring far-reaching changes to the way the force is run. But even the title frightens me. *The New Face of Modern Policing in the Urban Environment - Responding to Changes in the Community.* It sounds too much like a bloody Home Office initiative. Change, yes, of course. But what the position paper suggests is no less than a total re-evaluation of the philosophy of policing.'

There was something in the DCC's voice that Mallory picked up. 'It's not just the changes, is it?'

'You're right, of course. Even allowing for change, it's the underlying management philosophy that worries me most of all. Look what's happened to some social services departments. They've been assessed and they've ticked all the right boxes. As a result, they've been graded as excellent. But it's all just theory. In practice, that grading bears no resemblance at all to what actually happens on the ground when it comes to, say, looking after vulnerable children. Because too many of them fall through the net. No, I'm sick and tired of hearing that everything should be joined up, cost effective in its use of resource deployment and management-driven. Because all it does is it makes things look efficient. On paper.'

'So what exactly will these changes involve?' Mallory asked, shocked at the venom in the DCC's voice.

'A complete restructuring of the force, particularly the command system. And one of the first casualties will be the senior management group. Which I happen to think is the most effective way of running the force. But then I would, wouldn't I, since I set it up.'

'What's the chances of the position paper being implemented?'

The DCC shrugged. 'Some of the recommendations will happen whether or not Minter is appointed. But I think the chief constable feels that bringing in an outsider to head the reorganization is a necessity to shake off old attitudes.'

'And will he be appointed?'

'Ah, the big question. If the chief constable can get the Police Authority and the mayor's office on side he'll be able to control the way the force moves forward. No doubt about that. But before that happens, I fear a power struggle will rear its ugly head. What did somebody call it – a battle for the heart and soul of the force? And your role, David, could be pivotal.'

'My role?' Mallory sounded surprised.

'Yes. Crime management will sit at the centre of any new policing initiative. After all, it's why we're here in the first place. So what you have to do, is to be more forward looking in your planning. You have to formulate a strategic initiative that will map out the future direction of crime management, and which will take the ground from under the feet of those who support the position paper. But you'll have to be careful, because if you lose, it could be goodnight Vienna for your career.'

'Where does the Police Authority stand in all this?'

'With its present make-up, my guess is it's fifty/fifty. About half will accept the major restructure. But it's by no means a lost cause. You're widely respected, David. And if you come up with the right kind of strategy, we might win the day. So you'll have to take the initiative and I'll be happy to help there. And make no mistake, it's time to commit.'

'Do I sense a *but* in there somewhere?'

'Yes, a big *but*. Anything that shows the force in a bad light could be very dangerous at the moment. Particularly anything as high profile as the Faith Conference. The eyes of the world will be on Garton then, and if anything goes wrong it'll be the highest profile fuck-up you've ever seen. And from what I understand this religious madman, the *God Slayer* as the media call him, has already taken out the three principal keynote speakers. Good God, man, in itself that would be more than enough for the organizers to consider cancelling the conference. And I think they might have done if the chief constable and the mayor's office hadn't told them they could guarantee security at the conference. And that'll only work, David, if you get the madman who's going around killing religious leaders. Before the damage becomes too much to contain.'

'So the pressure's on?'

'Pressure? You'll get pressure from all sides. From the chief constable, from the senior management group, from the conference committee, from the mayor's office, and from the media. Believe me, living in Garton over the next few days will be like trying to survive in a pressure cooker. And as I said, the only way to relieve that pressure is to catch the madman.'

13

As the team gathered for the next morning's briefing, one of the phones on the table rang. Falcon took the call and identified himself. Then he listened for a moment.

'Thanks. Bring her to the major incident room, will you?'

He replaced the receiver and turned to Mallory. 'A young woman has just turned up at the main desk saying she thinks she knows where the monk's robes came from. The ones worn by the killer.'

'How does she know about them?' Fiona asked.

'Apparently, she saw them on TV.'

Falcon was about to ask something else when an officer brought a young woman to the operations room and introduced her as Debbie Connelly.

She was in her late twenties, Fiona guessed. Tall, slim and dressed with a casual elegance in designer jeans and a denim blouse.

'Miss Connelly.' Mallory moved forward. 'I understand you have some evidence on the uniforms used in the murders of the religious leaders?'

'Yes, I think—'

Mallory interrupted her. 'At this stage, we don't know the nature of what you are about to tell us, and I'm obliged to ask you if you require to be legally represented?'

'No.' She shook her head, 'I don't think so anyway.'

'Good. We'd like to conduct an interview, but you can suspend it at any time if you feel you'd like a lawyer present.'

'OK.'

'I have to leave for another appointment now; Detective Chief Inspector Falcon will conduct the interview.'

Falcon stood up. 'If you will come with me, Ms Connelly, we'll use one of the interview rooms.' He turned to Fiona. 'I'd like you to be there.'

He led the way to the suite of small interview rooms overlooking the far end of the dais. Inside there was a table bolted to the wall with a jug of water and two glasses on it. Four plastic seats were arranged around the table. The only other furniture was a trolley with recording equipment on it.

Falcon waved Debbie Connelly to a chair. 'You are not under caution, and we'll treat this as a voluntary witness statement. But we would like this interview to be recorded. Do you have a problem with any of that?'

'No, I don't.'

'Just one other point, Dr Nightingale is a forensic psychiatrist employed by the police on the investigation. We would like her to be present throughout this interview and to ask questions if she sees fit to do so. Do we have your permission for this?'

'Yes, I don't mind. It just all seems a bit formal, that's all.' Her voice had a slight northern accent.

Falcon smiled. 'Times we live in, I'm afraid. Evidence can be discounted later if everything isn't made crystal clear at the start of an interview.'

He walked over to the trolley, inserted two tape cassettes into the recorder and switched the machine on.

'*The Garton Police Investigation into the murders of the religious leaders. Witness Statement from Debbie Connelly on Tuesday, the 14 April, 2009. Time, 09.15. Interview held at Garton Police Headquarters. Present, Debbie Connelly, Chief Inspector Falcon, Garton CID, and Dr Fiona Nightingale, a forensic psychiatrist on the staff of the Waring Special Hospital who is acting on behalf of the Garton Police. Ms Connelly is here voluntarily and is not under caution. She will be informed if her status changes as the result of anything she may reveal during the interview. She has also been advised of her right to a lawyer, but has declined to be legally represented.*'

Falcon came back to the table and sat opposite Debbie Connelly, with Fiona next to him.

'OK, so that's the formalities over with. Now, I believe you have some information on the robes used by the killer in what's become known in the media as the God Slayer murders.'

'Yes, once I saw them on TV, I recognized the robes worn in both murders.'

Falcon didn't say anything about the third murder, preferring the interview to gather its own momentum.

'When did you realize this?'

'When I was watching the local TV news this morning.'

'You say you recognized the robes. So, I take it you've seen them before.

'Yes, I have. Or at least, robes that were very similar to them.'

'And where was this?'

'Let me explain. I'm an actress, and my latest part was in a film in France. But that was a lucky break, and for most of the last two years I've been what we call in the business 'resting'. Some of the time I spent in London, but I'm from the village of Langley, just outside Garton, and when I'm short of funds I come home and stay with my parents. I did that after the film in France. When I was home I became friendly with the local vicar, Sebastian Banks, when I was helping with a Sunday School nativity play. Anyway afterwards Seb told me he'd found the costumes and stage directions for an old mystery play hidden in the crypt of the church. Apparently, the Langley Mystery Play was a famous event in the Middle Ages. But after the village had suffered from the plague, the play seems to have been forgotten. But Seb had the idea to revive it and make money for the church, which needs a new roof. And he asked for my help.'

'What exactly is the play?' Falcon asked.

'Like all street theatre of this type it was a very stylized version of good triumphing over evil. In the play, the warrior monks fought the enemies of Christ, who were represented here by the Jews and the Muslims. Not very PC, of course, but good theatre. In the final scene St George slew the dragon, or "the serpent of old" as its sometimes called.'

'The serpent of old?' Fiona repeated the words.

'Yes, the Devil. Or Satan. Seb told me that in Christian symbolism the Devil was often represented by a dragon.'

Just as Professor Brinton had explained, Fiona thought.

'Tell us a bit more about the warrior monks,' Falcon asked.

'There were three types in the play. From the three major orders, Seb said. The Knights Templar, the Hostpitallers and the Teutonic Knights. And they were dressed in full costumes, chain mail and everything.'

'And you say the costumes were hidden in the crypt of the church?'

'That's right, and they'd obviously been there for some time because they needed extensive repairs.'

'Did anyone else, apart from you and the vicar, know about the costumes?'

'I don't think so; Seb wanted to be sure he could revive the play before he made anything public.'

'Which would account for the fact that no one else has come forward and identified the robes.' Falcon fought to keep the excitement out of his voice. 'One more thing: did the monks have weapons?'

'Yes, they did, and quite fearsome they were too. Swords, mainly. Oh, yes, and lances with banners attached to them.'

'What was on the banners?'

'Dragons.'

'I think we should go and pay this vicar a visit.' Falcon was finished now.

'Ah, you could just have a problem there, I'm afraid. I went to see him as soon as I recognized the robes on the TV. But he wasn't in, and apparently he hasn't been seen for a few days.'

'Did you get to know Sebastian Banks well when you were working on the play with him?'

She gave a small, almost secretive smile. 'He was' – she hesitated – 'becoming interested in me. It was early days, but I think he would have liked our relationship to grow.'

'How far *had* the relationship developed?' Falcon asked.

Debbie turned away, thinking. 'We'd been out for a meal a few times, and to the theatre in Garton. And the last couple of times we'd kissed at the end of the evening. So the relationship was gaining momentum, but it's still in the early stages.'

'Thank you Ms Connelly. We might need to speak to you again, but for the moment that will be all. A constable will help you with your written statement. And thank you again. For the tape, the interview is concluded at 09.34.'

As soon As Debbie Connelly left with the constable, Falcon asked Sergeant Maltravers to initiate a full background search on Sebastian Banks, Vicar of Langley. Then he looked at Fiona.

'Are we on the edge of a breakthrough here?' he asked.

'Well, we learned a great deal from Debbie Connelly. And most important of all, we can now set the murders into context. The warrior monks, the sham swordfights, the dragon banners. All these are typical street theatre. If the theme of the play that the vicar found is typical of its kind, then good will prevail over evil. But our killer has changed that around. I think he's been acting out his own version of the mystery play and this time the Devil triumphs. And you're right to concentrate on the vicar, because we might just have found the God Slayer.'

14

The church of St Bartholomew was on the side of the green in the centre of the small village of Langley. Built in the fourteenth century, the church had a rich history and had been the centre of life in the village for generations. But, like many churches, its importance had declined in the recent past as the old rural life had fallen away.

Falcon had opted for a softly-softly approach and a single unmarked police car pulled to a stop in front of the gates leading into the churchyard. But it was smoke and mirrors, because the entire village was sealed off by road blocks.

Nothing in, nothing out.

Except for the armed response and dog units, waiting to be called on if necessary. But as it turned out, Debbie Connelly had been right. Both the church and the vicarage behind it were deserted, the vicar nowhere to be found. So the road blocks were lifted.

A small crowd gathered as the gates to the churchyard were sealed off by police tape. As the villagers watched, a stream of vehicles rolled up, disgorging police reinforcements and the scenes-of-crime team. For the rest of the morning and into the afternoon the police carried out a detailed search of the vicarage and the church grounds. Then they started on the church itself.

Fiona had been attending a patient management review at the special hospital in the late morning, but she'd asked to be present as soon as possible after scenes-of-crime had carried out their preliminary survey of the church, and Falcon arranged to have her brought to Langley by police car. When she arrived, the crowd on the village green had been swollen by the media, who'd appeared as soon as the road blocks were lifted. This was national news and TV film crews were collecting background shots and interviewing any locals they could find.

Inside the church it was cool and dark, the stained-glass windows throwing coloured shafts of light onto the flagged floor. Fiona followed Falcon along the aisle to the rear of the altar. A heavy, iron-studded wooden door in a side wall was open and a SOCO took them down a flight of steps into the crypt. Lights had been rigged up down there, and technicians were taking photographs and searching for evidence.

'Over here.' Arthur Fielding, who headed up scenes-of-crime, called to them. He was standing in front of a large chest. It looked very old, Fiona thought, the wood dark with the patina of age. The top was open, the heavy hinges rusted now.

'This appears to be the store for the pageant material we were told to look for. We're doing an inventory now, and you can see the articles later, but it doesn't look to me as if there's much in here.'

'Thanks, Arthur. Anything else at this stage?' Falcon asked.

'Not a lot. Apart from the old chest, there's nothing of note down here. Except for that passage in the far wall.' He pointed to a hole in the wall which had a pile of stones by the side of it. 'At some time the entrance had been closed off with sandstone blocks, and it looks as if it was only opened up recently.'

'How can you tell that?' Falcon asked him.

'The wisdom of many years of experience.' Fielding grinned.'Oh, and the fact that there's an electric hammer chisel behind the pile of stones.'

'What's on the other side?'

'Just another room. Smaller than the one we're in now, but empty. The only things of interest are a patch where the cover of dust is thinner than on the rest of the floor and some scuff marks. The size of the patch corresponds to the size of the chest, and I'd say it's been moved from there. And for the moment, that's about it. We'll get back to you when the inventory of the chest contents is complete.'

*

61

Outside, it had started to rain, a gentle spring drizzle that stuck to clothes.

'Sir.' A uniformed officer came up the path and spoke to Falcon. 'There's a man at the churchyard gate said he'd like to talk to you.'

'What about?' Falcon asked.

'He just said that he might be able to help with your inquiries.'

Fiona and Falcon walked back down the stone-flagged path to the gate. Another uniformed officer was standing there by the scenes-of-crime tape. A man in cords and a denim shirt was waiting by his side. He came forward as Falcon and Fiona approached.

'Jack Davies. It doesn't take a genius to link all this' – he swept his hand to take in the village green – 'to the recent murders in Garton, and I thought I might be able to help with local background. I used to be in the job. DI in the Met. Came here for the peace and quiet of the rural life.'

Falcon grinned and held out his hand. 'DCI Falcon, Garton CID. And this is our offender profiler, Fiona Nightingale.'

They shook hands. 'How long have you lived in the village?' Falcon asked.

'For the last eight years. The way things work around here that doesn't exactly make me a native. But I'm halfway to being accepted.'

Falcon blessed his luck at finding a ready made source of information into life in Langley. Especially one who'd been in the job.

'Thanks for your offer of help, Jack. And we should talk. So, how about we use the interview room in the mobile operations centre? Give us some peace and quiet.'

Falcon took Fiona and Jack Davies over to the caravan that was fitted out as an operations centre and climbed the steps to the door. Then he turned to Jack Davies.

'Jack, this is not a formal interview, it's just a chat. But I'd like to record it so we can come back to it later if we need to. Is that OK.'

'No problem.'

Falcon walked over to a cubicle at the far end of the caravan. Inside there was a table top bolted to the side wall and supported on a single leg, with four plastic chairs arranged around it. A tape recorder stood on the table, with a pack of tapes beside it. Falcon tore the plastic covering off two of the cassettes, inserted them into the recorder, switched the machine on and recorded the interview identification formalities.

'OK, Jack, thanks for agreeing to help with our inquiries. First off, you said you had lived in Langley for eight years. Do you play any part in the running of the village?'

'Yes, I'm a member of the parish council, and I'm on the committee of the bowling club. My wife's in the WI and the flower club. And we're both regular members of the church. So I guess you could say we've fitted in here.'

'Great. Now, as you quite rightly guessed, we're here as part of the investigation into the religious murders in Garton. It follows a visit we had from Debbie Connelly who recognized the monks' uniforms the killer had worn. She said they were part of the costumes for the Langley Mystery Play that the vicar had asked her to help re-stage. So, of course, we were very interested in the vicar, but Debbie Connelly said he'd recently disappeared. What can you tell us about Sebastian Banks?'

Jack Davies took a moment to gather his thoughts together. 'In a number of ways he wasn't your bog standard village vicar. A bit "other worldly" really. He had good academic qualifications, maybe too good for a parish priest, but he handled his duties well enough and he was popular.'

'Is he married?' Falcon asked.

'No, he lived in the vicarage with his sister. She also had a religious background and had spent time in Africa as a missionary. A couple of years ago she returned to Africa, and Sebastian went out there to work with her for a spell. He came back, but she's still out there now. I know the details because it all came up on the parish council.'

'Who ran the church when the vicar was away?'

'The archdiocese used to send vicars from the neighbouring parishes for the religious festivals, and everything else was covered by the two parish deacons. But it's all going to change soon anyway. There's going to be a big reorganization in the archdiocese in the next few months. Parishes shared, churches closed and vicarages sold off.'

'Where does Langley fit into all this?'

'We didn't fare well, I fear. It was to be one of four local parishes served by a single vicar. Where he was to be based hadn't been decided, and the parish council mounted a campaign to have the vicar working out of Langley.'

'So, as the incumbent vicar, Sebastian Banks led the fight to save his church?'

'Not exactly.'

'How do you mean, not exactly?'

'Well, when he came back from Africa he seemed a changed man. Deeply introverted. Difficult to get close too. As if there was some weight pressing down on him. To the extent that at one stage he went to the church for counselling.'

'How do you know that?'

'He was very up-front about it, and for a while the counselling seemed to work and he became more like his old self. Then someone suggested that staging the old Langley Mystery Play would give the church a high profile. The idea seemed to revitalize the vicar and he started to research the play. From what he told us later, he'd found a mention in some old records that the script for the play, and the costumes used in it, had been hidden in a sealed-off part of the crypt. Apparently, he'd gone down there and eventually he'd found a blocked off room with an old wooden chest that contained everything that had been used to stage the play.'

'Did any of the parishioners see the material in the chest?'

'Not as far as I know. The vicar wanted to keep everything under his hat until he could be sure the mystery play could be re-staged, and Debbie was helping him with that.'

'But why was it hidden away in the first place?' Fiona asked.

'Apparently, towards the end of the seventeenth century, the local lord was a strict Quaker who took grave exception to anything like mystery plays, and threatened to destroy everything to do with the Langley play. So it was hidden, and it stayed buried until Sebastian Banks found it in the crypt of the church.'

'You said earlier that the vicar was different when he came back from Africa. How did this show?' Fiona asked.

'As I said, he was always introverted, but he was a kind man who would go out of his way to help his flock. But after Africa he seemed to shut himself off, and he did seem troubled.'

'Troubled?'

'Yes, once or twice one of the deacons would find him praying, spread-eagled on the floor in front of the altar. And there were rumours that he prayed deep into the night sometimes.'

'But you said he came back to his old self after counselling?'

'There was an improvement, yes. But I don't want to give the impression that he returned to his old self.'

'And now he's disappeared,' Fiona said softly.

'When exactly did he go missing?' Falcon asked.

'I can't be sure because the fact that he wasn't seen on a particular day doesn't prove he wasn't around anymore. I do know that he didn't attend the parish council meeting two days ago. I went round to the vicarage to give him some papers after the meeting but there was no one in.'

'So Debbie Connelly was right when she said he disappeared a few days ago.'

'Yes, you mentioned Debbie. What exactly is her role in all this?'

'Well, for a start she implied that Sebastian Banks was her boyfriend.'

'Her boyfriend? No, that was a student whom she met when he came to see Sebastian in Langley.'

'She also told us that Sebastian Banks had asked her to help re-stage the play. After she'd returned from France.'

'France?' Jack Davies sounded surprised.

'Yes, she went there to be in a film.'

'She wasn't in France. She was an in-patient having treatment in a mental health clinic.'

15

'Debbie Connelly's been in a mental health clinic?' Falcon repeated the words.

'Yes, I know that because her dad and I are friends. We both support the Garton Gladiators Rugby League team and go to the matches together. And I can tell you Debbie's had a mental health issue for some years now.'

'What's the nature of the problem?' Fiona asked.

'I've no idea. Her dad wasn't keen to talk about it.'

'OK.' Falcon nodded. 'But do you know which clinic she was being treated in?'

'Yes, it was the Hayfield Clinic, in a village outside Birmingham. I know that because Debbie's dad asked to borrow my satnav to get there and I plugged the location in using the data on headed notepaper from the clinic.'

'Do you know if she was sectioned when she was in the clinic?' Fiona asked.

'No, she was a voluntary patient.'

'And did she stay for the course of the treatment?'

'I don't know.'

'But her doctors thought she was fit to be discharged back into the community?'

'They must have done, I suppose.'

Fiona thought for a moment. 'Jack, you've been in the job, and I'm sure you'll understand this request. But please don't let on to anyone that you've told us Debbie Connelly has been a patient in a mental clinic. And particularly not to Debbie herself, or her parents. OK?'

'No problem. And her parents are away on a world cruise anyway.'

At that stage Falcon terminated the interview.

'Jack Davies is a useful contact, and we may need his help again. But right now we have to work out how to deal with the fact that Debbie Connelly, our star witness in the investigation, has been a patient in a mental health clinic. Jack Davies said she was in a place called the Hayfield Clinic. Is there anyway of finding out what she was in for?'

'That might be difficult,' Fiona said. 'Most clinicians treating mental health problems are understandably reluctant to reveal details of their patients. And normally, of course, it's forbidden under the rules of patient confidentiality. I can contact the clinic and try to get details on Debbie's condition, but we may have to obtain a court order before anyone agrees to talk to us.'

'OK, so try the softly softly approach first, and if that doesn't work we can always go to a judge. But there's something else with Debbie Connelly, isn't there?'

'You mean that she misled us when she said Sebastian Banks was her boyfriend?'

'Exactly. Why would she do that?'

'For the moment, I don't know. Maybe she's just protecting her real boyfriend by keeping his name out of it. But one thing's becoming clear: Debbie is a complex personality.'

'So how do we treat her in the meantime?'

'I have a suggestion there.' Fiona said.

'Go on'

'We know that she has been in a clinic, but she herself chose not to tell us that. In fact, she went out of her way to say she'd returned from filming in France. So if she is to be of any use to us, it's important that she doesn't find out that we're aware she has mental health issues. That's why I asked Jack Davies not to let it be known that he'd told us she had been in a clinic.'

'I wondered why you'd asked that.'

'It was so we could continue to use Debbie. If she found out we knew about the clinic she could well clam-up.'

Falcon thought for a moment. 'So far, mental condition or not, Debbie Connelly has supplied us with some very important information. And there's no question of any mischievous conduct on her part. At least, not so far. She's done nothing to pervert the course of justice, and she hasn't wasted police time. Quite the contrary, in fact. She was the one who pointed us to the warrior monk uniforms, and then gave us the name of the man who might very well be our prime suspect in the murders. The vicar, Sebastian Banks. So I suggest we bring Debbie Connelly in for another interview. But still not under caution, at least not at this stage, because that might frighten her off.'

'And what do we hope to find out at this interview?' Fiona asked.

'Why our star witness is playing mind games with us.'

16

Falcon found Debbie Connelly in the small crowd of villagers standing around the churchyard gate. She waved when she saw him and called out.

'Hi, Chief Inspector. Glad I could help your investigation earlier. Anything else I can do?'

'Thank you. I'd appreciate it if you'd agree to another interview. In the caravan if that's all right?'

'Sure.' She sounded almost effusive. 'Shall we go?'

Falcon took her to the caravan where Fiona was waiting in the interview cubicle. As soon as Debbie saw Fiona, her expression changed and a look of something close to malevolence crossed her face. But it was a fleeting shadow, no more.

Falcon went through the formalities of setting up the interview, and switched on the tape recorder. Then he sat down facing her.

'OK, Miss Connelly. Thank you for agreeing to a second interview.'

'No problem. And it's Debbie, by the way.'

'Debbie it is then. First off, let me say we found what you told us at the last interview very useful.'

'Glad to be of help.' She was almost purring, Fiona thought.

'Good.' Falcon smiled. 'What we'd like to do now is to find out as much as we can about Sebastian Banks. In your first interview you told us that you were helping him put on the mystery play.'

'That's right, I was.'

'And you also told us you were getting quite close to him.'

'Yes, I was.'

'So how did Sebastian Banks seem during the last few weeks?' Fiona shifted the emphasis of the questioning. 'I mean, did he appeared troubled by anything?'

'Troubled?' She made the word sound aggressive. But then she smiled. 'Not that I know of, no.'

Fiona remembered what Jack Davies had told them; that the vicar was a deeply troubled individual who had dramatically changed after returning from Africa. So troubled that he'd received counselling from the Church. Was it likely that he'd kept all this hidden from Debbie Connelly? Or didn't she really know him at all? Fiona couldn't answer that question yet, but she decided to keep probing.

'What did you think when he disappeared?'

'I didn't really know what to think.'

'OK, you didn't know what to think when Sebastian went missing. Understandable. But you felt worried enough to tell the police that you thought the robes worn by the God Slayer came from the mystery play. Robes that only you and Sebastian Banks knew about. So you must have had at least a suspicion that he was involved in some way in the murders.'

'I suppose I did think that, yes.'

'Can we just pause there for a second.' Falcon held up his hand. 'You knew that Sebastian Banks had access to the costumes, and you knew he'd disappeared. Both of those were enough to make you suspicious. But, and think carefully here, please, was there anything else about Sebastian Banks that made you think he might have committed the three murders? Anything he might have said, for instance?'

'Sometimes he did seem a bit. . . .' She hesitated, groping for the right word. 'A bit apart.'

'But you've already told us he didn't appear troubled.'

'No, I don't think he was so much troubled, it was more as if he'd shrunk into his own world.'

'And what kind of world was that?' Fiona asked.

'It was private. Somewhere he retreated to.'

'How do you mean, he retreated into this world?' Fiona felt it was time to push a little.

'Sometimes he'd be talking to you quite rationally, the next he'd be away to another planet. That sort of thing.'

'I see.' Falcon seemed happy to leave it at that for the moment, and he switched the emphasis of the questions. 'Debbie, have you any idea where he might have gone to?'

'I've thought about that because I knew you'd ask the question. And there was somewhere he once mentioned. He called it his sanctuary.'

'And where is it?' Falcon leaned forward across the table.

'I'm not sure, but. . . .'

'Yes,' Falcon bore in.

'He said it was a very old place that he'd found by following a series of instructions which were hidden in the stage directions for the mystery play.'

'Let's be absolutely clear on this.' Falcon held up a hand. 'According to you, Sebastian Banks followed a series of instructions hidden in the mystery play to find this "sanctuary"?'

'Yes.'

'But you don't know where it is?'

'No.'

'So to find it we have to unravel the play, and then follow the instructions ourselves if we want to reach Sebastian Banks.'

'It looks that way, yes. I might be able to help there because I studied the stage directions with Seb. And as an actress I might be able to see things in it that someone without a theatrical background might miss.'

'But you didn't pick up anything when you were working with him last time,' Falcon said.

'No, but I wasn't looking for hidden secrets then, was I?'

'True,' Falcon conceded the point.

'So if I went through the stage directions again, following the same procedures we used last time, I might be able to identify what Sebastian found there.'

'The mystery play,' Falcon said softly. 'First, the monks' robes, now some kind of hidden sanctuary.' It was beginning to seem that everything led back to the mystery play.

As Falcon escorted Debbie out of the caravan, Fiona stayed

behind in the cubicle, trying to make sense of her impressions. During the interview, even when Fiona was asking the questions, Debbie Connelly seemed to be replying to Falcon, almost as if Fiona herself wasn't there. In some ways that wasn't that unusual if Debbie was the kind of girl who liked to impress men.

Perhaps I'm imagining things, Fiona thought. But then she remembered the look of malevolence on the girl's face. Fleeting, or not, it had been real enough. Fiona was convinced of that.

But she had no idea what was behind it.

17

Fiona put the phone down and smiled to herself. Lance was still in the Falklands, but just the sound of his voice had been enough to lift her sprits. But the feeling was fleeting, and as she gazed across the river, she felt the uneasiness return.

Lance Monkton was a professor in the School of Earth and Ocean Sciences at the university, and they had first met when he'd given a public lecture at the Garton Museum. He was an impressive figure; tall and slim, his craggy face and cleft chin framed by a mass of dark curls. And he was good company, Fiona acknowledged that.

From that first meeting there had been a spark between them. But Fiona had deliberately kept him at arm's length, afraid to let him get too close because there was a part of Lance Monkton that he kept hidden. It was something to do with his past. But he always clammed up when she'd come anywhere near to it almost as if there was a section of his life that he'd thrown a fence around. Whenever the subject came up he switched moods and almost became another person.

He was aware of it and of the damage it was doing to their relationship, and several times he'd appeared to be about to open up. But he'd always pulled back at the last minute.

Fiona felt the problem with Lance was somehow just part of a general malaise that had plagued her for the last few months. A time when she'd found herself re-evaluating her life.

After medical school in Edinburgh, she'd opted to go into psychiatry, a decision she'd never regretted. The key turning in her career had been the time she'd spent at Father David's clinic. In many ways Father David was her mentor, the teacher who had guided her and carefully refined her approach to forensic psychiatry. He was a Catholic priest with a small ministry in Stamford. He was also a highly qualified psychiatrist who'd designed several internationally recognized programmes for the rehabilitation of patients suffering a variety of mental problems. He ran a clinic attached to a hospital run by nuns, and Fiona had spent two years working there.

Those two years at the clinic had been the hardest of Fiona's life. So much to learn, so much to understand. And Father David had opened her mind in a way she'd never thought possible. In psychiatry his thinking was extremely modern, even 'edge-of-the-science' in many respects. And he profoundly influenced Fiona's development, steering her into the field of rehabilitation therapy.

After the two years working with Father David she'd moved to a clinic in New England, where she specialized in offender profiling. It was while she was there that she met Craig, an ex-US marine turned novelist on the faculty of a nearby university. They had been very much in love and had looked forward to a lifetime together until the night Craig was murdered by a drug user when he was out jogging. Although she had gone through a succession of men, Fiona felt that she could never get over Craig. To compensate, she'd built a shell around herself, and within it she'd focused on the twin pillars of her career; offender profiling and rehabilitation therapy. And in both fields she had built up an international reputation, telling herself that her career was enough. But cracks were beginning to show in her carefully constructed façade even before Lance came onto the scene.

Fiona was having dinner that evening at her grandmother's house. The Nightingales had been an important family in Garton for over 200 years. Their shipping business had been sold off after the Second World War, but the family had retained their reputation as great social reformers, 'merchant philanthropists' who were fervent believers in the welfare state and had played a prominent role in the development of the city. Charlotte Nightingale, Fiona's grandmother, was an independent thinker and had been one of the first women to graduate in Social Science from Garton University. In the years between the wars she had served on the local council and on various bodies that struggled to obtain better conditions for women and children in the city. She had a great sense of family, a belief in the position of the Nightingales in the city, and still carried on her charity work.

For years now she had dropped hints of wanting great grandchildren while she was still able to enjoy them. She'd eyed every 'suitor', as she still called Fiona's menfriends, as a prospective husband, and she had positively drooled over Lance Monkton.

The dinner was a get-together for a number of people Charlotte was currently wooing as potential sponsors for a modern art exhibition she wanted to run for one of her charitable causes. It sounded as if it might well be a stultifying evening, but Fiona had to admit that her grandmother's dinner parties were seldom dull, and she was almost looking forward to it. At least, it would be a break from the investigation.

She dressed carefully, choosing a simple, but elegant, black dress, contrasted with a brightly pattered shawl. When she'd finished getting ready, she looked at herself in the full length mirror set into one of the doors in her wardrobe.

She was of medium height, slim but with a good figure. Her face had high cheekbones, a finely chiselled nose that was tilted at the tip, and a mouth that was really too large. All framed in shoulder-length dark hair.

Not for the first time she grinned as she looked at her reflection in the mirror. She was no Miss World, she thought, but she was comfortable with her looks. By the time she was ready to go out, the sense of melancholy she had felt had practically disappeared. But then her thoughts returned to Lance and a tiny part of her mind told her to be careful. There was no getting away from the fact that their relationship was flawed by some secret in his past.

And she couldn't help wondering what would happen on his return.

18

There was a sense of cautious optimism as Mallory addressed the morning briefing session.

'Sometimes in cases like this we get a breakthrough, and right now we might just be lucky.' He turned to Falcon. 'I know it's early days yet, but can you summarize what we've got that puts the Reverend Sebastian Banks in the frame?'

'First, he had access to the costumes used in the three murders. They're part of a mystery play that Banks was trying to re-stage. The costumes are old and made to a medieval design. So it's very unlikely that there'd be any other sets like this one around. Second, it appears that something happened to him when he was working with his sister in Africa. We don't know the details yet, but it was serious enough for him to undergo counselling and it might have sent him off the rails. Third, he disappeared from sight at about the time of the third murder. It's still all fairly flimsy, I agree – particularly the bit about his state of mind – but right now, Banks isn't just our prime suspect, he's our only suspect.'

'Right.' Mallory nodded. 'For now, we tag Sebastian Banks as our prime suspect. So the first priority is to find him. Now, according to Debbie Connelly, Banks asked her to work on the mystery play with him. And from what she told us, Banks followed a series of instructions in the script and found a sanctuary somewhere. Debbie is prepared to help us locate that place by going through the text of the play. I think she might respond better to another woman, so I'd like Sergeant Maltravers to delegate her present tasks and work with Debbie Connelly on locating the sanctuary that Sebastian

Banks found. A car's picking up Debbie in the next few minutes and bringing her here. Finding Sebastian Banks is top priority, so all the stops out, Sarge.'

'As you say, sir. All the stops out.' She lit up the room with one of her wonder smiles.

Sergeant Maltravers was tall, with a figure to kill for. And she had 'presence'. Innocent blue eyes and long blonde hair which she usually wore tucked demurely into a police hat that on her looked like a designer item. She was gentle and friendly, and was universally popular with both male and female members of the force throughout which she was known affectingly as Goldilocks. She was also a computer genius.

'Next,' Mallory continued, 'we need to establish as much background information as we can on Sebastian Banks himself. We've got uniforms out taking statements from everyone in the village, and they'll be collated and cross referenced. A tedious job, but we've got the new evidence correlation programme, UNRAVEL, designed by Sergeant Maltravers. We don't know how long you will be tied up with Debbie Connelly, Sarge, but I take it your team can run the programme?'

'No problem. They're all trained.'

'Fine. Next, we need to concentrate on Sebastian Banks's state of mind. Why did he need to have counselling when he returned from Africa? To find out, I've arranged with the archdiocese office for Gary and Fiona to interview the senior dean later this morning. All right?'

'No problem. But so we know who we're talking to, what exactly is a dean?' Falcon asked.

'I can answer that, one of my uncles was a dean in the Church of England,' Goldilocks said. 'A dean is a high-ranking cleric who runs a large church or a cathedral. This one, the senior dean, must be acting as diocese spokesman if they've lined him up to talk to us.'

'Thank you. But now for the bad news.' Mallory looked around, making sure he had everyone's undivided attention. 'We've identified Sebastian Banks as our prime suspect. And essentially, this was on the basis of evidence given by Debbie. And we were quite right to act on that evidence. But, and here's the problem, it appears that Debbie has spent time recently as a voluntary patient in a mental health clinic. So if it does turn out that she's a star witness, we need to know how far we can actually trust her evidence. Which means that we have to learn more about her mental health issues. We know the clinic she attended, and Fiona has agreed to talk to the doctors there and try to find out about her condition.'

Mallory stood up. 'Just one other matter for now, then. The media. How much do we give them at this stage? Fiona?'

'I think we should tell them that Sebastian Banks is wanted for questioning in connection with the murders of the three religious leaders. The media are poking around the village, and they'll find out soon enough that we've been looking for the vicar. So we might as well be up-front with them because the media coverage might turn up something that leads us to him.'

'So we make the search for Sebastian Banks public. A country-wide manhunt?' Falcon asked.

Mallory thought for a moment. 'Yes, we've enough evidence to do that. We might get our fingers burnt and look stupid if Banks just turns up, but, on balance, I think the positives outweigh the negatives. So, yes, a large-scale manhunt for the reverend.'

As they left the briefing Fiona was thinking about something Mallory had said. Something about how far they could actually trust Debbie Connelly's evidence. And Fiona couldn't help remembering the expression on the young woman's face.

Was she playing some game of her own? A game she was frightened Fiona would expose?

19

The atmosphere at the palace was sombre. Hardly surprising, Fiona thought, since the savage murder of the archbishop.

Fiona and Falcon were shown into the office of the senior dean of the cathedral by a middle-aged, conservatively dressed woman secretary who'd been working behind a desk in the ante-room.

The office was panelled in dark oak, with a series of gilt-framed portraits of past church dignitaries covering one entire wall. The opposite wall was lined with tall glass-fronted bookcases on either side of a stone fireplace. At the far end of the room, an ornate desk was set in front of mullioned windows. Two men were standing by the desk, one of them came forward as Fiona and Falcon entered the office.

He was wearing a grey shirt with a white dog-collar and a cross hung from a chain around his neck. He introduced himself as the senior dean of the cathedral.

'I'm Detective Chief Inspector Falcon and this is Fiona Nightingale, a forensic psychiatrist working with the Garton Police. Thank you for agreeing to see us.'

'Not at all, Chief Inspector.' He shook hands with them. 'You are welcome here, but I'm sorry the circumstances of the visit should be so terrible.'

He led them over to the front of the desk where two chairs had been placed.

'May I introduce Graham Stanhope? He's a lawyer representing the interests of the Anglican Church.' The man did not come from behind the desk but instead simply nodded, then sat down. He was tall and thin-faced, and had what Falcon described later as the expression of a suspicious fox.

'Please have a seat.' The dean indicated the two chairs, then went back around the desk and sat down himself.

Fiona realized then that the desk was on a slightly raised area so that the people behind it looked down on anyone sitting facing them, and she couldn't help thinking that there was something theatrical about all this, as if everything had been carefully staged to provide an advantage to the churchmen.

'Dean, we're here to ask some questions about Sebastian Banks.'

'And we are happy to answer those questions.' It was Stanhope that answered. 'As far as we can, that is.

'How do you mean, sir? As far as you can?' Falcon had obviously decided to establish the rules of engagement from the start.

'You must understand, Chief Inspector, that we may face issues of priest confidentiality here.' Stanhope smiled. Fiona guessed it was meant to be a reassuring gesture, but she noticed it didn't reach his eyes.

'And you must understand that this is a murder inquiry. As such, I expect all my questions to be answered. Before we begin, I need to know who you are, and why the dean wants you present at this interview.'

'I am, was, an adviser to the archbishop. My role now is to protect the interests of the Church.'

'You think those interests need protecting?'

'They may do, yes.'

'You are aware that I could hold this interview at police headquarters, if I wished?'

Stanhope sighed. An exaggerated sound. 'Yes, I'm aware of that.'

The testosterone was clearly switched on, Fiona thought, as each man sought to establish an advantage.

'I could also insist on taping this interview, but as a gesture to the Church I am prepared to waive that.'

'Gentlemen.' The dean had been watching the exchange. 'We are here to explore if there any ways we can help to throw light on these dreadful murders. This interview should not deteriorate into a slanging match. I'm sure the archbishop would not have wanted that.' A pause as the dean looked at the two men. 'And neither do I.'

There was an edge of steel in the words that seemed to come as much of a shock to Stanhope as to Falcon.

'That's perfectly clear, Dean.' Stanhope tried to gain some of the initiative, but the dean was having none of it. There were clearly other issues here, Fiona thought, and the dean was obviously determined to keep Stanhope on a short lead.

'I think I had better lay down some ground rules,' the dean went on. 'Of course the police may ask as many questions as they like. It could not be otherwise. If I require legal guidance on any particular question I will turn to you, Mr Stanhope. Otherwise your role here is that of an observer. No more than that, and only if the chief inspector agrees to your presence.' He looked at Falcon.

'No problem.' Falcon had gained what he wanted; to talk directly to the dean, and he was happy to let Stanhope remain.

'Now we've established that, perhaps we can begin.'

'Thank you, sir. Let me start by summarizing some new information we've gathered on the murders of the religious leaders.'

Quickly and concisely he explained how Debbie Connelly had made the connection between the costumes of the warrior monks and the Langley Mystery Play, and had then come forward to the police with her suspicions about Sebastian Banks. He also explained that Banks had disappeared, and that the police were looking for him. He finished by pointing out that the police had been told Sebastian Banks had undergone counselling from the church.

'Thank you, Chief Inspector,' the dean replied. 'I can well understand that you need to find Sebastian. But let me say at the outset, for the record, that the Church is not hiding him.'

'We don't believe that the Church is involved at all.' Falcon stressed the point to reassure the dean. 'We simply need to build a profile of Sebastian Banks. This is necessary both to track him down, or failing that, to predict how he might behave in the future.'

The dean nodded. 'Yes, I can see that. So how would you like the interview to proceed?'

'Perhaps I can come in here.' Stanhope sounded more conciliatory now. Anxious even, Fiona thought.

'I think a suitable way to proceed would be for the dean to tell you what he knows about Sebastian Banks. Then you can ask questions.'

'I'd like to confer with my colleague.'

Falcon stood up and walked over to the far corner of the office. Fiona followed him.

'This is getting to be ridiculous.' He kept his voice low. 'There's no way I can agree to giving control of the interview to Stanhope.'

Fiona nodded. 'I can understand your reservations, but unless you do agree, it's my guess that he will keep raising objections at every stage of the proceedings. And remember, you're very experienced at teasing out information at interviews. So let Stanhope have his way. Allow the dean to make his statement, which Stanhope has probably vetted anyway, then both of us can cut in with the questions. You never know, if they do have anything to hide, we may hit pay dirt this way.'

20

'Sebastian was a theologian.' The dean placed his fingers together in an arch. 'All priests are, of course, but in his case he had a genuine flair for academic scholarship. So much so, that I often thought he would have been more suited to a collage life in his beloved Oxford, than to being a pastoral priest. But there was something in him. A feeling of being called to the faith. Called to preach the Gospel to a flock. And indeed there was a practical side to his religion, so that he was well able to cope with the everyday running of a parish. The nitty-gritty of a modern vicar's life. And he was helped in his pastoral work by his sister, Margaret, who used to live with him in the vicarage until she went out to the Republic of Bwanda in southern Africa as a missionary.'

The dean was silent for a moment, arranging his thoughts.

'I said that Sebastian was called to preach the faith, and he felt there was something fundamental about missionary work, about leading uninitiated masses to a belief in Christ. That was why he took a sabbatical leave and joined his sister in Bwanda for a year. In a way, it wasn't the right time to leave his parish in Langley. Like many organizations, the Church periodically undergoes modifications and, to be truthful, Langley was about to lose its vicar and become a shared parish. Sebastian knew this, but he felt it his greater duty to undertake the missionary work rather than fight for the survival of his parish.'

'And the church authorities agreed to his sabbatical?' Fiona asked.

'Yes. In a way, I suppose we didn't oppose his leave because it meant there would be less opposition to the changes at home. But things moved too slowly, and nothing about the future of the church in Langley had been decided before Sebastian returned. So we all expected him to rally the troops as it were, and fight the changes. But that didn't materialize, because when he came back he didn't seem to have the heart for a fight. In fact, he was very much a changed man. He appeared deeply troubled, and that was the point at which he came to us for counselling. In fact, I was the one who led the counselling.'

The dean paused to pour himself a drink of water from a carafe on the desk.

'Following the usual pattern, we had several long discussions. It was during these sessions that it became increasingly obvious to me that Sebastian was suffering a deep crisis of faith, and I admit that I was shocked at the extent to which he had lost his belief. It would be no exaggeration to describe him as a lost soul wandering around in a dark universe. I tried to identify the cause of his despair, but when I found I was getting no further forward I referred him to another member of our counselling service who was specially trained for just such situations. After a number of preliminary sessions Sebastian went into retreat and it was there that the truth came out.'

The dean opened a buff-coloured folder that was lying on the desk top and extracted a single sheet of paper. He read through it, as if he was familiarizing himself with what was there, then he sighed.

'This is a very difficult situation for me. And indeed for the Church. It is made very clear at the start of counselling that the process is totally confidential. It could even be construed to fall into the protocol of the confessional where the priest is sworn to secrecy. And this is the point that concerns Mr Stanhope.'

Oh, no it's not, Falcon thought. Stanhope couldn't care less about confidentiality. He just wants to make sure that the Church doesn't get loaded with the blame for the killings. But Falcon kept his suspicions to himself for the moment, content to see how the dean would handle the issue.

In fact it was Stanhope who picked up the thread. 'What the dean is holding is a testament Sebastian Banks wrote during his counselling sessions. It has no bearing on your murder case, and it must therefore remain confidential.'

Falcon shook his head. 'You know very well that I can't simply take your word that the statement has no bearing on our investigation. You're just fishing. Nothing more. You don't want Sebastian Banks to be in the frame for these murders. But if you don't disclose the contents of that statement I'll get a court order forcing you to do so.'

'There will be no need for that, Chief Inspector.' The dean's voice had hardened again. 'There can be absolutely no suspicion that the Church is trying to protect a murder suspect, especially if that suspect is one of their own priests. No hint whatsoever. I will have a copy of the testament made for your files, together with any other relevant papers.'

He looked defiantly at Stanhope, but the lawyer remained silent.

'The crisis of faith suffered by Sebastian Banks was the direct result of something that happened while he was serving as a missionary in Bwanda. And I must say at the outset, that what took place was so shocking it would test anyone's faith. Sebastian's sister, Margaret, was working at a missionary station in the north of Bwanda, serving a parish that extended over several hundred square miles and was covered by a team of mainly African workers. In may ways, it was a successful mission and churches had been established in a number of key villages.'

'When Sebastian got there he expressed a wish to work among the villages in a strip of land running across the north of the country. Unfortunately, while he was there a civil war broke out in Bwanda. Essentially, the population consists of two main groups. The majority Tombas in the south, and the minority Kempas in the north. As often happens in this part of Africa, the split is on tribal grounds, but in fact it goes deeper than that. The Tombas have held power in the country for generations, and the largely agricultural Kempas have been more or less left alone to get on with their lives. But all that changed when oil was found in the north, in the part of the country occupied by the Kempas. At this point, the Kempas decided to break away and they declared independence. But the

Tombas wanted the oil and they invaded the north of the country. That was the start of civil war.'

The dean took another sip of water.

'It was a vicious conflict, with many acts of barbarism on the part of the Tombas. And Sebastian Banks was caught up in one such act. An act that shook his faith to its very foundations. So much so, he could not believe that a loving God would countenance such evil. And that was why he took counselling.'

'What was this act of barbarism that affected his faith?' Fiona asked.

'I think it would be better if you learned about it first hand from Sebastian himself.'

'But how can we do that, he's gone missing?' Falcon sounded puzzled.

'By reading his account of the incident in the testament which he wrote during his counselling.'

'What form did the counselling take?' Fiona asked.

'Counselling in this archdiocese involves a multi-faceted approach, if you'll forgive the jargon. Every person who accepts counselling is assigned a mentor, someone who will be available at all times, and the "treatment", if one may call it that, includes one-to-one therapy, and group therapy sessions, in which the applicant is encouraged to confront whatever problem troubles them.'

'And if they reach the stage where they are prepared to actually confront issues, what then?'

The dean looked at her and smiled. 'You are a psychiatrist, and I expect our approach is not very different from yours, In fact, we have trained psychiatrists available if needed. But in Sebastian's case, I can tell you that, among other things, he was encouraged to set his memories of what happened in Bwanda down on paper, and that is what you should read.'

He opened the buff file and extracted a couple of sheets of typewritten paper.

'As I said, I will have a copy made for you. I think you'll find it a harrowing document that goes a long way to explaining Sebastian's crisis of faith.'

'Thank you, I look forward to reading it.' Fiona said. 'For how long did he undergo counselling?'

'Almost a year. At the beginning he spent a month in sanctuary, but the rest of the time he was able to carry on with his parish duties.'

'Did he overcome his problems?' Falcon asked.

The dean sighed. 'I'm not sure anyone totally overcomes problems like those that faced Sebastian. But I'm sure he found at least some vestige of his faith again, and so were the people running his counselling. They felt they'd gone as far as they could, and the sessions finished. But the real question, I suppose, should be was Sebastian himself certain he had regained his faith.'

'And how would you answer that?' Fiona asked.

'I think he was still uncertain. To the extent that he looked for something that would test how far his faith had been restored. And he found such a test in a in a seminar on *Belief in Crisis* being run in the Faculty of Religious Studies at the university.'

'And how did this test go?'

'You'd have to ask the organizers of the seminar about that, I'm afraid.'

'Who was in charge of the seminar?'

'It was Dr David Perdue.'

'Just one more question,' Falcon said. 'We have information that Sebastian Banks has a sanctuary. Have you any idea where that might be?'

'A sanctuary?' The dean repeated the words, then shook his head. 'Sorry. I've no idea where that may be. No idea at all.'

21

Fiona and Falcon had a sandwich lunch at a country pub close to the Hayfield Clinic where Debbie Connelly had been an in-patient. Earlier, Fiona had contacted the director of the clinic over the phone, explaining that she'd like to talk to the doctor who'd treated Connelly. Once he realized the nature of the enquiries the director had agreed that she could come to the clinic, but had stressed that any decisions regarding the release of information lay entirely with the patient's doctor.

The clinic was in the countryside to the north of Garton, a modern purpose-built facility funded by the private sector. It was a low security environment and when Falcon announced their arrival into a squawk box, the barrier across the car-park entrance lifted. Inside the building they reported to the reception desk where Dr John Martin was waiting for them.

The doctor was tall and thin, in his middle thirties. They shook hands, then he led them into a pleasantly furnished lounge and showed them to chairs around a coffee table in front of a window overlooking a garden.

'Thank you for agreeing to see us,' Falcon kicked off. 'And let me make it clear from the start that I'm fully aware of the constraints you are under with respect to giving up medical evidence.'

'Thank you, that will make things a good deal easier. But before we talk, let me get one thing clear: do you suspect that Debbie is involved in the murders of the religious leaders in Garton?'

'We don't think she's directly involved, no. It's simply that she provided us with certain information that might lead us to identify the killer.' Falcon was choosing his words carefully. 'But because we have learned that she has mental health issues, we need to know how far we can trust her evidence.'

'That is what the Director of Medical Services at the clinic told me after Dr Nightingale had contacted him, and because of the seriousness of these killings the director agreed that I might provide you with certain information that would usually remain confidential. But for anything else, although the clinic will be very happy to co-operate, you must provide a court order – to safeguard our position.'

'I understand,' Falcon nodded. 'But I would like to record the interview – to safeguard our position.'

'No problem.' Dr Martin grinned. 'So much safeguarding, I'm surprised you're allowed to ask anything in interviews.'

'Tell me about it.' Falcon made a face as he set up the recording equipment he'd brought with him. 'Sometimes I'm afraid to ask a suspect the time of day, in case his brief takes exception. There.' He slid two blank tapes in to the recorder, and went through the identification process.

'Ready. Now I'd like to pass over to Dr Nightingale.'

'Hi.' Fiona smiled. 'I don't think we've met, have we?'

'No, I've only been in post a few months after coming down from London. But I am aware of your work. And I must say, it's very impressive.'

'Thank you.' Fiona smiled again. 'So first off, can you confirm that Debbie Connelly was a patient at this clinic?'

'Yes, she was.'

'And what was her status?'

'She was an in-patient on a voluntary basis.'

'And you were her Responsible Clinician?'

'Yes, although I still find the new title a bit odd. As far as I'm concerned RMO was quite sufficient.'

Fiona nodded. 'Change for the sake of change, I agree. Now, can you tell us the nature of Debbie's condition?'

'In general terms, she suffers from an "attention seeking syndrome"?'

'And how long was Debbie a patient here?'

'Pass. For that you need the court order.'

'OK. I assume you had full access to her records?'

'Yes, of course.'

'So, is there anything you can tell us about her history?'

'I am able to tell you that she had been known to psychiatric services, off and on, since she was a child. It was always on a voluntary basis, and her condition has never been serious enough to warrant putting her under section.'

'Thank you. Now, if you hadn't read her records, would you still have diagnosed her as suffering from an attention seeking syndrome?'

'Yes, on the basis of her presentation I was able to confirm the earlier diagnosis.'

'Did you have reason to believe that her condition was becoming more acute?'

'As I said, I had not known her before. But during the therapy sessions I did come to the conclusion that her condition was deteriorating.'

'What was the evidence for this?'

'I can't go into that I'm afraid, not without the court order.'

'But her attention seeking was getting worse?' Falcon was trying to make sense of what the doctor was saying.

'Yes, I believe it had become a deep seated need that was beginning to dominate her life.'

'But she'd lived with it up until then, hadn't she?' Falcon asked.

'She'd more or less come to terms with her condition, yes. To put it simply, she'd achieved that by becoming an actress which had fulfilled her need to seek attention. Once she was up there on the stage in front of an audience, she felt she was someone. There's a danger in that, of course, because make-believe can take over from reality. But with Debbie, the first big hurdle to overcome was that she really wasn't very good at acting. At least not good enough to reach the top.'

'And she realized this herself?' Fiona asked.

'I think she did. Being on stage, even in minor roles, seemed to satisfy her craving for attention. Paradoxically, I would even say that Debbie had become reasonably well adjusted.'

'Then why did she feel the need to undergo further treatment?'

'That is the crux of the matter, and I can't answer it, I'm afraid. Not because I refuse to, but because I simply don't know. She did believe she needed further treatment, that much is obvious and, as we moved forward, it became apparent that something had happened in her life. Something that had shattered the safe boundaries that she'd constructed around herself over the years. But every time we got close to the problem, she shied off.'

'So you felt you'd gone as far as you could and you discharged her?' Falcon asked.

'No, she was a voluntary patient and she discharged herself.'

'So why did she admit herself to the clinic in the first place?' Falcon was becoming more and more confused.

'I think part of her genuinely wanted to understand her condition. To get back to the safe times she knew previously. And in a way, I think that trying to get back to those safe times in her teens, when she was protected at home, was maybe the key to the whole of Debbie's problems. But, as I said, as soon as we started to make progress she backed off.'

'But why did you suspect that Debbie's condition was deteriorating? Can you tell us anything at all about that?' Fiona asked.

'All I can say is that I believe something had burrowed so deep down in her mind that this time, no matter how hard she tried, in the final analysis she was afraid to confront it.'

22

Falcon brought the evening briefing up to speed on what they'd learned from Dr Martin at the clinic.

When he'd finished Mallory tapped his fingers on the table. 'So Sebastian Banks remains our prime suspect, but, as we feared, our chief witness has serious mental health issues.' He turned to Fiona. 'Can you tell us a little bit more about this attention seeking syndrome that Debbie Connelly suffers from?'

'A very common form of attention seeking is when a child is naughty simply to gain the attention of adults. But, in fact, there's a whole spectrum of symptoms, right up to Munchausen Syndrome by Proxy where a patient will actually cause harm to someone else as a means of gaining attention.'

'Do sufferers have any symptoms in common?'

'Each case is unique, of course, but often attention seekers have a low sense of worth, or self esteem if you like, and are emotionally insecure. But, as I said, the condition covers a wide range of symptoms, and I can't make a long range judgement of Debbie Connelly.'

'But nothing showed up when we interviewed her?'

Fiona was silent for a moment, remembering the malevolent look on Debbie Connelly's face in the mobile operations centre the day before. But she shook her head. 'Nothing obvious. No.'

'So how do we treat her now?'

'A good question.' Fiona thought for a moment. 'We have a witness. But we know now that she's an attention seeker. So we have to face the possibility that she came to us to put herself centre stage by making it appear that she is essential to our investigation. But she doesn't know we are aware of her condition, so I suggest we treat her the same as we would any other witness, and hope that she really can assist us with information on Sebastian Banks.'

'How would she react if she found out we know about her problems?' Mallory wanted to be quite clear on the point.

'I think she'd simply clam up on us, and look for some other way of grabbing attention.'

'So you're saying let's use her before that happens?'

'Yes, that's exactly what I'm saying.'

A few minutes later Sergeant Maltravers joined the briefing.

'Sorry I'm late but when Debbie's in full flight it's difficult to stop her.'

'No problem,' Mallory told her. 'We've picked up a few things about Debbie that you should be aware of, and DCI Falcon will bring you up to speed on those later. For now, can you give us a progress report on the search for Sebastian Bank's hideaway?'

'Surely.' Goldilocks smiled. 'I spent all day with Debbie going through the Langley mystery play. I offered to go to her home, but she preferred to work here, at police headquarters, and I found us a small office. As I said, I've just come from there and I'll write a full report later. But I can give you the bones now.'

'Go ahead.' Mallory told her.

'The main thrust of our investigation centred around the mystery play, because Debbie told us that Sebastian Banks had followed a series of instructions hidden in the play to find his sanctuary. And I must say, Debbie knows her stuff. So much so, my head's spinning. Let me see now.'

She opened an A4 notebook and turned to the first page. 'Mystery plays dramatize events in the Bible, and are different from miracle plays that concentrate on the lives of the saints. Mystery plays are essentially a medieval art form, and many were run by the craft guilds. Famous ones still going are found at Chester, Wakefield, York and several smaller towns and villages. Originally, they were performed to illustrate Bible stories to the people because services in those days were said in Latin, a language in which most common folk weren't versed in.'

She turned to the next page of her notes.

'Although the plays are not all the same they do tend to have a common theme, and that's the battle between good and evil, which was much more a part of life in the days when the plays were first staged than it is now. Most of the plays centre around episodes from the Bible, such as the Creation, the Flood, Moses, the Nativity, the Last Supper, the Crucifixion and the Resurrection and were usually put on around the summer feast of Corpus Christi. The plays are performed as street theatre, sometimes from specially decorated wagons that were dragged to audience sites. So that's the general background.'

'You seem to know a lot about the subject,' Mallory said.

Goldilocks sighed. 'Believe me, Sir, I've had hours of it, and that's just the bones.' She turned over a few more pages in the notebook.

'Now we do actually come to the Langley mystery play. It seems that originally, the monks in Langley Abbey wanted to provide the people of Langley with illustrated Bible stories and they devised the play. It went round the village in procession, and stopped at various locations on a circuit where wagons were positioned. Essentially the episodes illustrated in the play were the Creation, the Nativity and the Crucifixion. Then later, in the fifteenth century the play was modified to make it much more of a showpiece by introducing a number of battle scenes. These were related to two themes. One, as far as historians believe, was based on the story of Sir Gawain and the Green Knight and the other on the legend of St George and the Dragon. Although it later became embroiled with the age of chivalry, apparently St George and the Dragon was a story originally brought back to Europe by the Crusaders and that was how it was treated in the Langley mystery play, as another battle in the good versus evil scenario with the dragon representing Satan. In the play itself, the monks of war fight the Saracens then St George slays the dragon. The reason for the inclusion of the story of Sir Gawain and the Green Knight in the play is apparently not clear, but is somehow related to the time the plague hit the village, although all the dates apparently got mixed up somehow. And that about sums up where we are today. Which, with respect to finding Sebastian Banks, is exactly zilch. Do you want to continue with this, sir?'

'First question, do you think Debbie Connelly is deliberately stringing things out?' Mallory asked.

'Difficult to say, but she told me that she didn't know where to find the instructions leading to Sebastian Banks's sanctuary in the play, and the only way forward was for the two of us to study the stage directions in detail. And to do it properly we needed to understand the background of the play. So I suppose there's a kind of sense in her approach.'

'What do you think, Fiona?' Mallory didn't sound convinced.

'Debbie may well be stringing things along to make herself needed and stay in the limelight. We just don't know. But for the moment, I suggest we let her move at her own pace. Which means Sergeant Maltravers will have to have more sessions with her, I'm afraid.'

Goldilocks sighed again and made a face. 'I can't wait.'

23

Fiona was sitting in semi-darkness, watching the lights of the ships on the river. It had been a long day but she couldn't relax, and she let her thoughts run free to explore all aspects of the three murders.

Then she switched on a lamp and picked up the red folder that the dean had given her. She opened it and extracted two A4 sheets of paper fastened together with a paper clip. She leaned back in her chair and started to read the testament Sebastian Banks had written when he was being counselled.

'I had been up country to visit a newly established Christian community close to the border. I stayed there for three days and it was when I returned to our headquarters church that the attack happened.

I was driving the Land Rover and there were two others in the vehicle with me; a local nurse and a United Nations doctor. We were about fifty miles from the village when we crested a rise and saw the gun-ships.They were circling in the sky above the position of the village and suddenly we saw flashes and columns of smoke rose into the air. Several times the gunships circled the area before they went away, leaving dark clouds behind in the sky. To reach the village we had to descend into a steep sided valley and we were out of sight of what was happening for almost an hour as we followed a boulder strewn track. Then we climbed out of the valley and entered that world of carnage.

I have played that scene through my mind in countless nightmares, or in the dark times when sleep would not come to me. In those nightmares I am there again. I can see it. I can smell it. The sickly sweet odour of charred flesh that drifted on the smoke-filled air. And the birds, huge vultures, slowly circling on the air currents. Waiting their time.

It was clear from the damage that the gunships had been followed by troops on the ground. Nothing it seemed, had been spared in that terrible wasteland. This village would never recover because there was nothing left. All the huts were burned to the ground; the water pump was smashed and the well blown up; the animals were slaughtered; the few pitiful patches where crops had grown were churned into no more than red earth now. But one thing was absent in that place of desolation.

People.

The only substantial building in the village was the church. Built with funds raised by the missionary society, it was constructed out of breeze block, with a corrugated iron roof. As we drove into the village, smoke was pouring from the shattered glass of the windows, and hanging on the air.

Something seemed odd, out of place. Then I realized what it was. The door to the church was closed. It was a heavy wooden door lovingly carved with simple Biblical scenes by a local craftsman. It was famous, that door, and had featured on the front cover of several African missionary magazines. It was a symbol of Christian worship, and it was always kept open, whatever the time of day, to welcome worshippers inside.

Now, it was closed. Held shut by heavy planks nailed into the doorframe. And, as I switched off the engine of the Land Rover, I heard the sounds. Low, choked sounds, as if they were coming from a long way off.

The Land Rover carried a survival kit in the boot and I took a claw hammer from it and loosened the planks holding the door closed. One by one I prised them off, then pulled the door open.

I don't know what I expected, but in the clouds of swirling smoke I could see that the church was deserted. Completely empty, the rows of wooden chairs gone, leaving an empty space where tendrils of smoke swirled around. And the noise, louder now that we were inside the church. It seemed to come from the far end of the building where a trap door led down into the cellar beneath the church. It was used to store food and medical supplies in a safe place.

But on that afternoon it had been put to another purpose.

A long heavy bench had been pushed on top of the trapdoor and we had to drag it away, coughing in the smoke emerging from the edges of the door. With the weight of the bench gone, the trapdoor sprang open as if a great pressure had been released. The air which escaped was thick with the acrid smell of petrol and charred flesh. And, worst of all, bodies appeared, their limbs intertwined in the struggle to get out of that place.

Below them, at the top of the steps more bodies were crushed into unnatural poses as they had been forced against the door by the people under them trying to fight their way out, the crush so bad that we couldn't see into the cellar. But, as the trapdoor was pulled back the bodies began to slip down, moving in a kind of grotesque ballet as their limbs came free. In the light from the church that filtered down we saw into the depths of the cellar. And the scene that was revealed in the half darkness will live with me all my days.

The cellar was stacked with bodies; men, women and children, completely covering the beaten earth floor. Layer upon layer of them. Those at the top of the piles had taken the brunt of the flames as the petrol had been ignited and the flesh had been boiled off their bodies. But those below had not been spared because, as we found out later from the pitiful few who survived, soldiers had stood on the steps and fired round after round of bullets into them.

Of all the people of the village only eight came out of that charnel-house alive. The rest were dead. Massacred in the name of . . . what?

A loving God?'

For a long time Fiona just sat there, lost in the horror witnessed by Sebastian Banks. Little wonder it had turned him against religion. And now he was the prime suspect for the killings.

Well, Fiona thought, he certainly fits the profile. A man who's lost every ounce of faith he ever had, and is driven now to take revenge on the God that has deserted him.

And yet.

The dean had told them that Sebastian Banks thought he had recovered his faith to the extent that he was prepared to test himself by participating in a seminar on *Belief in Crisis* at the university – to show others the way back to salvation.

A grim paradox.

24

The next morning Fiona rang the Department of Religious Studies at the university and asked to speak to the faculty member who had organized the *Belief in Crisis* seminar. She was put through to Dr David Perdue who agreed to see her and Falcon later that morning.

The Department of Religious Studies was in the old part of the university and when Fiona checked in at the office a secretary rang Dr Perdue who came to meet them. He was short and portly and, with his bald head and rosy cheeks, Fiona thought he bore a striking resemblance to Mr Pickwick in the Dickens stories. After he'd introduced himself, he took them to his office and ushered them inside.

Like Professor Brinton's office, it was a typical academic's room; floor to ceiling shelves crammed with books, a large desk with a computer on it, and beyond that a small coffee table and chairs arranged in an alcove under a window.

'Would you like coffee? I've just made some,' Dr Perdue asked, his voice sounding as if it echoed from a pulpit.

They agreed that coffee would be very welcome and waited as Dr Perdue filled three mugs from a percolator on the table by the widow. Then they sat down around the table.

'So, how can I help you?'

'Fiona, please, and thank you for seeing us. As I explained when I asked for the appointment, Detective Chief Inspector Falcon is a member of the Garton Police Force, and I am a psychiatrist retained by the force. We're both working on the religious killings.'

'Dreadful business. Dreadful. I knew all three victims.'

'You knew them personally?'

'You shouldn't be surprised. The Department of Religious Studies covers all the major faiths. My own speciality is medieval Christianity, but the school plays a vital role in all religious affairs in the city.'

'Do you train people entering the Church?' Falcon asked.

Dr Perdue shook his head. 'No, our degrees are strictly of a secular nature, although many of our students do eventually go on to take holy orders.' He sipped his coffee. 'Now, over the phone you said that you're looking into the background of Sebastian Banks.'

'That's right,' Fiona nodded.

'And now you say you're working for the Garton Police on the so-called God Slayer murders. So I have to ask, do you believe Sebastian is involved in the murders?'

Falcon answered. 'We think that he may be *connected* to the killings, and we're looking into his background.'

'Then why not talk to him directly?'

'We can't do that, I'm afraid.'

'Why not?'

'Because he's disappeared.'

'I see.' Dr Perdue was silent for a moment. 'Can you tell me the nature of the evidence that you believe connects Sebastian to the murders?'

'I can tell you that he had access to the costumes worn by the killer.'

'The monks of war outfits, you mean?'

'Yes.'

'And that's it?'

'It's all I can say at the moment. That and the fact that he's disappeared. And it's his disappearance we've really come to see you about. We wondered if it's connected to his crisis of faith the dean at the cathedral told us about.'

'You've spoken to the dean?'

'Yes, we went to see him yesterday. He said that Sebastian Banks had suffered a crisis following an incident that happened while he was on missionary duty in Africa. The dean also provided us with an account of the incident Sebastian had written during his

100

counselling sessions.'

'Then the dean must have thought it very important, because releasing anything at all revealed during counselling involves a grave breach of confidentiality.'

'I think the dean wanted the church to be seen to be co-operating in the investigation of the murders, and he told us about the crisis of faith because he thought that it may have a bearing on Sebastian Banks's behaviour.

'As an act of revenge against religion?' Perdue sounded shocked.

'We don't know, and that's why we've come to see you. Because Sebastian apparently gave a lecture at a seminar you held in your department on *Belief in Crisis*.'

'Yes, it was one of our regular seminar series, and Sebastian did give a lecture, two in fact, as part of the programme.' Perdue was clearly struggling to come to terms with the idea that Sebastian Banks might be a murderer.

'How well did you know Mr Banks?' Falcon asked.

'We were colleagues. Sebastian has a strong academic interest in the history of the Church, particularly the medieval Church. As I said before, that's my own field of interest and we worked together on a number of occasions.'

'Did you knew him personally, as well as professionally?'

Dr Perdue hesitated. 'Well, actually, no. He was never one for close friendships. Oh, I don't mean he was standoffish, it was just that he didn't allow anyone to get close to him. But as I said, as colleagues we worked together.'

'And the seminar,' Falcon asked. 'Was it you who suggested he gave the lectures?'

'Yes, I invited him personally.'

'Who attended them?'

'A whole spectrum of people. Third year degree students, M.Sc. and Ph.D. students and any local clergy, or come to that, members of the public, who wanted to come. Attendance varied on different days, but I'd say an average of around fifty were present at each lecture.'

'And what about Sebastian Banks's lectures? Did you attend them personally?'

'Yes, I did. Both of them.'

'And how did they go down?'

'Very well. He spoke about what happened to him in Africa, and he was quite candid about the way it impacted on his faith.'

'Did he give you the impression that he'd come through his personal crisis?' Fiona leaned forward in her seat.

'To be quite honest, I'd have to say his recovery was very much a work in progress, and perhaps that was what made his two lectures so popular. I think the audience could sense that a battle still raged inside him. In fact, when I think about it, that theme of fighting a battle came out in the discussions following Sebastian's first lecture. It happened when one of the people there challenged him. And it was then that Sebastian's doubts began to resurface. Almost as if—'

'As if what?' Fiona pushed the question.

'As if all the counselling he'd had was being destroyed. Or, at least, severely challenged.'

'And was this just one person who challenged Sebastian? Or was the entire audience involved?'

'No, the audience wasn't involved. The discussion, I almost said fight, was between the two of them.'

'And who was this other person, do you know?' Fiona asked.

'Oh, yes, it was Mark DeMasters. One of our final year honours students who's—' Perdue hesitated again.

'Who's what?'

'Who's gone missing. Just like Sebastian Banks.'

25

'How long has he been missing?'

'I don't know.'

'So how do you know he's actually gone missing at all?'

'He applied to do a masters degree, and he was awarded one of the prestigious scholarships. But he didn't turn up when the awards were published and, strictly speaking, the award offered to him has lapsed now. I know his personal tutor, Chris Barfoot, was most surprised when Mark didn't show up to accept the award.'

'Personal tutor. Is that something different from an academic tutor?' Falcon asked.

'Yes, a personal tutor offers advice on things such as general welfare and finances. All the non-academic issues facing a student. Hang on a minute, Chris's office is just down the corridor. I'll see if he's available.'

Doctor Perdue went outside and when he came back there was another man with him. He was in his early thirties, and was wearing an open neck check shirt and jeans.

'This is Dr Barfoot, Mark's personal tutor.'

Fiona shook his hand and introduced herself and Falcon. 'Thanks for agreeing to see us, Dr Barfoot.'

'Chris, please. Normally, I wouldn't discuss a student without their permission. But I understand from David that you two are from the police, and that you're making inquiries about Mark DeMasters. If Mark's in trouble, then I'll be happy to help as much as I can.'

Fiona caught something in his voice. Something that suggested that he wasn't totally surprised that Mark DeMasters might be in trouble.'

'So tell us about him,' she asked.

The four of them sat down around the coffee table and waited for Chris Barfoot to speak.

'Mark's a strange character, although after the kind of upbringing he had perhaps it's not so strange at all. His father was a religious bigot who terrorized his family for years.'

'What church did Mark's father belong to?' Fiona asked.

'He didn't belong to any of the established churches. From what Mark told me, none of them would have given him houseroom. He was far too much of a fanatic for that. A fire and brimstone character who saw sin everywhere. By profession, he was a schoolteacher, and apparently as far as his work was concerned he seemed quite normal. It was in the family setting that the other side of his personality came out.'

'Not unusual,' Fiona said. 'One face to the world, another to the family. So what was the face he presented to the family?'

'Well, for one thing, he kept them isolated. Oh, the kids went to school, but that was about it. The two of them, Mark and his younger sister Isabel, had no real friends. There were no visitors to the house, and the kids weren't allowed to play out. In fact, I don't think they were allowed to play at all. Everything in the house was structured around the Bible. But by all accounts it was a very strict interpretation of the Good Book. From what Mark told me, "spare the rod and spoil the child" didn't even get close to the way they were brought up.'

'You mean the father used to beat them?' Falcon asked.

'Oh, yes. Quite regularly. Anything that violated the rules of the house, was chastized by what sounded almost like ritualistic punishment. And it wasn't just beatings. Apparently, one of the father's special punishments was to shut one of the children into a hole he'd dug in the garage of the house. It was closed off by a trapdoor and he would keep the children in there for days if he thought they'd gone against him. And it wasn't only the children who suffered. Their mother was also subjected to what amounted to a rule of terror. And that included physical abuse apparently.'

'Did she try to stop what was happening to the children?' Falcon put the question.

'At the beginning she did what she could to control his excesses, but as they got worse she seemed to give up, and even appeared to support him in the end.'

'Again, not an unusual behaviour pattern,' Fiona nodded. 'Over time, she probably became more and more blunted until there was little of her original personality left. To have given in would have been an easy way out because it would have stopped her having to think. Having to use energy fighting back. Until in the end, she probably came entirely under his spell. Total dominance in other words.'

'And this went on right through Mark's childhood?' Falcon asked.

'Yes, until he went to university.'

'What kind of student was he?' Fiona asked.

'A very bright one. His undergraduate thesis was one of the best we've had in years. And after graduation this summer he wanted us to take him into the Masters Programme. In fact, he applied for a prestigious scholarship and won it against severe competition. That was when we were aware he'd disappeared, when he failed to formally accept it.'

'What about his lectures? Wouldn't he have been missed there?' Falcon put the question.

'Not at this time of year, no. Most of the courses have finished, and the students are revising for exams.'

'We understand from Dr Perdue that Mark attended lectures given by Sebastain Banks at a seminar on loss of faith. Can you tell us anything about that?' Falcon asked.

'The discussion, or I suppose it was actually an argument, started in the questions session at the end of one of the lectures.'

'What was the nature of the questions?' Falcon pursued the point.

'So as far as I can remember they all revolved around the extent to which a person could regain faith after a traumatic experience.'

'And that's what they argued about?'

'Yes.'

'Did they maintain contact after the seminar?'

'I saw them having coffee together in the student cafeteria after the last lecture, but I don't know if they met later.'

'When you saw them having coffee did they seem to be carrying on the argument?'

'Now that's a strange thing. No, they seemed quite friendly.'

'Do you have a photograph of Mark?' Fiona asked.

'Yes, there will be one in his record file,' Dr Perdue replied. 'All students have to provide one when they register in their first year. I can get you a copy if you like.'

'Thanks, that will be helpful. And we'd like his address too.'

'No problem. Do you want his home address as well as his address here in the university?'

'He lived in the university?'

'For his final year, yes. The faculty have a small student residence here on campus. It's old, part of a monastery that was on the land originally taken over by the university. It's mainly for post-graduate students, but Mark was allocated a room there while he worked on the paper he had to submit for the scholarship.'

'Can we see the room, please?' Fiona asked.

'Of course. Perhaps you can take them, Chris, while I get the photograph copied.'

The room was in a stone-flagged passage overlooking a cloistered garden. Chris Barfoot had borrowed a key from the porter's lodge, and he opened the heavy wooden door.

Inside, the room was austere. Almost monastic, Fiona thought. The walls were plain plaster, painted white, and apart from a bookcase to one side of a small stone fireplace, the only furniture was a bed and a desk and chair under the window.

They were standing at the open door, and Fiona started to move inside. But she stopped as she heard Chris Barfoot gasp. He was transfixed, his eyes locked on a cross over the fireplace. Not an unusual possession in the room of a student studying religion, Fiona thought.

Except this one was upside down.

26

'Adding in everything you've got so far, can you sketch a profile of the killer?' Mallory put the question to Fiona at the start of the evening briefing.

Fiona nodded. 'A full profile, no, not enough information for that. But I expected the question, and I've prepared a set of notes. I've only had time to write them on an acetate for now, but I'll tidy them up and put them on PowerPoint later.'

To start with she brought Mallory up to speed on the meetings at the cathedral and the university. Then she walked over to a projector standing on a trolley positioned in front of a screen.

'Everything we've learned so far points to the killer being a person of deeply held religious views whose faith has been severely challenged recently, challenged to the extent that he's become a killer who's exacted revenge against all established religions. So let's see how Sebastian Banks might fit this partial profile.'

She switched the projector on and placed an acetate sheet on the surface. There were only two bullet points written on it.

1 - Sebastian Banks suffered a crisis of faith following an incident that occurred when he was a missionary in Bwanda - which could fit our profile of the killer:
2 - Sebastian Banks underwent counselling arranged by the Church, and from what both the dean and Dr Perdue told us, his recovery was still a work in progress - which could also fit our profile of the killer.

'So you're happy for Sebastian Banks to remain as our prime suspect?' Mallory asked.

'Yes, I am. Despite the fact that he appears to have come some way towards reconciliation, I sense that he's still a deeply disturbed individual. Even though we still have to remember that as yet we've no hard evidence against him, or against anyone else, come to that.'

'But for the moment, we concentrate on Sebastian Banks.'

'Yes.' Fiona was adamant on that.

'So what about the new face on the block? This Mark DeMasters? Is he part of the picture?' Mallory asked.

'Sebastian Banks met him at a seminar on Belief in Crisis in the Religious Studies Department at the university. Mark DeMasters is a final year student in the department. Apparently, he had a strange upbringing in a home dominated by a father who was a religious fanatic. We know the two of them, Banks and DeMasters, met after the seminar because they were seen drinking coffee at the university. But we don't know how far the relationship developed. We do know, however, that like Sebastian Banks, Mark DeMasters is a troubled individual. If for no other reason than we found a cross hanging upside down in his room. And what might be extremely important is that both Sebastian Banks and Mark DeMasters have disappeared, although we can't link the two disappearances.'

'OK, so we can't link them yet. But are you even suggesting that this Mark DeMasters might be involved in any way in the killings?' Falcon came in with the question.

Fiona shrugged. 'I don't know. But there's definitely something odd about him. The inverted cross we found in his room, for one thing, because from what Chris Barfoot told me that's a deliberate anti-Christ image. A symbol that demonstrates Mark DeMasters has turned his back on the Church.'

Mallory began to pace the floor. 'So both men had good reason to question their beliefs on the basis of things that happened to them in the past. Banks because of the events in Africa and DeMasterrs because of his twisted upbringing. And apparently they argued with each other at the seminar. Anything else?'

'Not apart from the fact that they appear to have disappeared at about the same time.' Fiona replied.

'And where does Debbie Connelly fit into the picture?' Mallory asked.

'We can't be certain. But don't forget, she came to us of her own free will to volunteer information on the robes worn by the monks. And it was Debbie who first brought Sebastian Banks into the picture. So, at this stage, I think her role is simply that of an attention seeker. Helping the police by making out she's a critical witness puts her centre stage. In other words, she's an observer looking in.'

'She doesn't pose any kind of threat?' Mallory asked.

'With what we know about her at this stage, I'd say no,' Fiona answered.

'So we have three names in the matrix,' Falcon said. 'Sebastian Banks, Mark DeMasters and Debbie Connelly. All apparently troubled souls. But which one is capable of murder?'

Falcon walked over to a whiteboard and drew three large circles on it. Then he wrote a name in each circle.

'We can link Debbie Connelly and Banks because they'd been working together on the mystery play.'

He drew an unbroken line joining the two circles together.

'We can also link Banks and DeMasters because they met at the seminar where Banks was speaking.'

He drew another unbroken line joining the circles with Banks and DeMasters' names inside.

'But at the moment, we can't directly link DeMasters and Debbie Connelly, either with each other, or with the village of Langley.'

He drew a third, this time broken, line joining the circles with Debbie Connelly and DeMasters inside. In the break in the line he drew in a large question mark.

'But wait a minute,' Falcon interrupted. 'Didn't that DI from the Met tell us that Connelly's boyfriend was a student she met in Langley?'

'Yes, he did.' Fiona agreed. 'You think that student could be Mark DeMasters?'

'A bit of a coincidence otherwise,' Falcon said. 'But to check it out we can use the photograph of DeMasters that the university supplied. I'll get copies made and have them shown around

Langley. Maybe someone will have seen him in the village.'

'Good idea. Get onto it as soon as the briefing's over. Now' – Mallory turned to Sergeant Maltravers – 'are you any further forward with the search for the hiding place that Banks might be using?'

Goldilocks looked around the table. 'No. But trying to find it from instructions hidden in the play was always a long shot. We knew that.'

'And you got nowhere?' Falcon wanted to be absolutely certain.

'Nowhere at all.' Goldilocks lit the room with one of her smiles. 'But I do know a lot about medieval mystery plays.'

'Thank you, Sergeant.' Mallory couldn't help grinning. 'So, let's summarize. We have three people in the matrix. Sebastian Banks, Mark DeMasters and Debbie Connelly. But as Fiona pointed out, at this stage we don't have one scrap of hard evidence against any of them. Everything's purely circumstantial. Now, before we finish I'd like DI Logan to report on a development in the possible role of the Jewish sect in all this. Dan?'

Logan nodded. 'Aaron Levi told us that a sect of orthodox Jews from the States believe that a great treasure was hidden somewhere in the James Street synagogue during WWII. So I increased the surveillance around the synagogue, and we picked up six adult males dressed in the style of orthodox Jews entering the building late this afternoon. The point here is that although there are some orthodox Jews living in Garton they don't use the James Street synagogue. So a party of six entering the synagogue dressed in the orthodox fashion was unusual enough to set alarm bells ringing and I'm in the process of putting someone on the ground in the area.'

'What about Aaron Levi? What does he have to say about it?'

For a moment Logan didn't answer.

'Dan.'

'Look, whatever the Guardians are doing in the synagogue has a religious aspect and frankly, guv, I'm not sure whose side Aaron Levi will be on if we question him. For the moment I'd rather keep him on the sidelines until we have to use him.'

'OK, I'll go along with that.' Mallory nodded. 'Anything else?'

'One thing. As soon as the Guardians came onto the scene I initiated a check with immigration to see if the group had come in through any of the usual channels, and it appears they entered the country via Manchester airport late yesterday from the States.'

'Thanks, Dan,' Mallory said. 'So for the moment we seem to have covered—'

He was interrupted as a constable came onto the platform and approached him.

'There's a Debbie Connelly at the front desk, sir. Says she has some vital information for you.'

'Bring her up, Dan, can you turn the whiteboard around please? We don't want Debbie Connelly to find out she's a suspect in the investigation.'

27

'Sorry about this.' Debbie Connelly placed a leather satchel on the table in front of Goldilocks. 'But something came to me after we'd finished this afternoon. And I think I've cracked the code hidden in the play.'

Goldilocks looked towards Mallory and, when he nodded, she opened the satchel and extracted a thick volume. It had a richly decorated deep-blue board cover and was closed with a metal clasp.

'I've not seen this before.' Goldilocks sounded puzzled.

'That's right.' Debbie smiled. 'Neither had I until an hour ago. When you'd gone I remembered that we'd seen some notes that had been added to the stage directions, in the way a modern theatre director might make notes on the script of a play. But then I wondered if anyone would actually deface an original illustrated manuscript. So I went back into the room in the crypt and I found this in a false bottom of the old chest that the rest of the stuff was found in. It's the original script for the play. The one we've been using is simply a working copy.'

'And the original copy is different?' Goldilocks asked.

'Yes, it's much more detailed and the illustrative work is quite outstanding. In fact, if Seb wanted money for his church he could have raised tens of thousands, maybe even hundreds of thousands, by selling a medieval illuminated manuscript of this class in this condition.'

'And you say you've located Sebastian's sanctuary?'

'Yes, I think I have. It's all in the manuscript. And I know Seb found the book because there were paper strips at various places in the text with notes written on them in what I recognized as Seb's handwriting. So I can take you through the text. I'm sure we shouldn't actually be handling a manuscript of this value without taking all sorts of precautions, but I suppose it's all right under the circumstances.'

She looked across at Mallory.

'This is evidence now and we can't wait for an expert to show up. So be careful, but open it.'

Goldilocks gave Debbie a pair of latex gloves, and when she'd pulled them on she lifted the heavy cover and opened the book. It was gilded in silver and gold, and for a moment everyone around the table was caught by the sheer beauty of the illustrator's work. Then Debbie Connelly turned a few pages and pointed with her finger. 'Look, this is the first chapter. It starts with a decorated initial, that's the large letter in a square which covers half the page. The copy also had initials, but they were much simpler and didn't have images inside them like the original does. And these initials are the key to understanding the hidden nature of the play, which is to provide directions to the sanctuary.'

'But why should it be hidden in the first place?' Mallory asked.

'I can answer that from Seb's notes. He'd found out from a search of the parish records that during the Black Death of 1348, the monks of the Langley monastery, which is just a small community now, had sought sanctuary from the plague in the surrounding forest. When the plague passed them by they built a chapel on the site to give thanks for their deliverance. Apparently, they felt their salvation was a sign from God that showed they had been chosen, above all the other people in the area, to survive, and the chapel was hidden because they thought the plague might return and they wanted to save the site exclusively for their own use.'

'Not what one would expect from men of God.' Falcon said.

'Don't forget these were the times of the plague when all sorts of meanings were given to its visitation,' Debbie Connelly said.

'And you say you've located the site of this chapel?'

'Yes, the clues are embedded in the decorative initials at the chapter heads. Let me show you.'

She pointed to the initial at the start of the first chapter. 'The main image is a pictorial representation of the monastery. It's highly stylized, with towers and a moat, but that's not unusual in this kind of manuscript. Then you can see a number of knights gathered around the monastery. Knights, not monks. But look at this one, here.'

She pointed with a finger.

'This knight's dressed in a suit of armour with the visor in his helmet in the raised position. He's carrying a shield with a red cross on a white background and he's holding a sword. But like the other knights, he's on foot.'

She carefully turned several pages. 'Then in the square at the start of the second chapter, the knights are on horseback and are riding away from the monastery. You can see the knight with the red cross is at the front.'

She turned more pages. 'Then in the following chapters the number of knights gradually reduces, until finally our friend with the red and white cross is the only one left. Then we follow him on various stages of a journey which ends when he enters a forest and reaches a chapel set among the trees. Again, it's a very stylized pictorial version of a chapel with intricate ornate stonework. Like something out of the legend of Camelot. But it's the next picture that's significant.'

She turned more pages.

'There. In this square, our knight is clearly underground. You can see the ground itself with the sky above it, and a cave beneath. The knight's in the cave, and he's back on foot now standing in front of a river. I think that's more symbolism, made to look as if the knight is about to cross into another world. But if you look carefully you can see an altar with a golden chalice on it in the bottom right-hand corner of the square. The chapel the monks built in celebration of their salvation was underground, and I think the knight's in there. In the illustration.'

'And you believe that's where Sebastian Banks is hiding out?' Falcon asked.

'Yes, I do,' Debbie Connelly replied.

'An underground chapel built by monks who'd survived the

plague hundreds of years ago, and who hid the directions for finding the place in an old manuscript.' Mallory grinned suddenly. 'You must admit, it does sound just a little far fetched.'

'It does.' Debbie grinned back at him. 'But it shows these things don't just happen in the movies.'

Mallory decided he was definitely not going down that road. 'But we still don't know where this chapel is.'

'Oh, I think we do. Look.' Debbie Connelly pointed to the ground above where the knight was standing. 'That rock formation. It looks like a lion crouching down. It's pretty unusual, and I think it's meant to pinpoint the entrance to the chapel.'

'So let's get back to reality for a moment. We suspect that Sebastian Banks is hiding in an underground chapel located in the vicinity of a particular rock formation. So let's see if such a rock formation actually exists, and isn't just a figment of the imagination of some medieval scribe. Sergeant, any ideas?'

'What's the forest called?' Goldilocks asked.

'Langley Woods,' Debbie answered.

'Is it a tourist attraction?'

'Yes, the place is crisscrossed with hiking trails, and in the middle there's a lake with water sports.'

'OK, let's see if it has a website.'

Goldilocks stood up and crossed the dais to one of the computers. She sat down and booted it up, then keyed Langley Woods into the search engine. The screen displayed a website with a number of photographs on it. The central photograph was of a lake surrounded by forest. It had been taken in bright sunlight with sailing dinghies and canoes on the lake surface. There were several other photographs around the centre image.

'That's it.' Goldilocks pointed to a picture of a rock formation, where the limestone was shaped into an outline of a crouching lion.

Mallory thought for a moment. 'So the rock formation does actually exist, which means we have to check it out. But it's getting dark outside now and we don't want to go blundering around in the half light. On the other hand, we can't risk letting Banks slip away. So I'll contact the monastery to let them know what's happening on the their land, then I'll send in a rapid response unit to stake out the area until the morning.' He turned to Debbie Connelly. 'Thank you very much for all your help. It's much appreciated.'

'Oh, is that it? You don't want me there when you locate Seb?'

'No, it's strictly a police matter now. But, I would like you to make a full statement detailing everything you put together. Sergeant Maltravers will take you into one of the interview rooms and assist you. We'll let you know what happens at the chapel and, as I said, many thanks for your help.'

Mallory looked at Fiona when Debbie Connelly and Sergeant Maltravers had left.

'Any thoughts?'

Fiona walked over to the whiteboard Falcon had been using and stood in front of it. 'Sebastian Banks, Mark DeMasters and Debbie Connelly.' She muttered the words to herself. 'Which one is the ringmaster?' she asked.

'Any preference?' Falcon asked.

'I would say that Sebastian Banks is the most likely candidate. He could well have appeared as a father figure to Mark DeMasters.'

'And Debbie Connelly?'

'Ah, there lies a mystery. I was surprised when Debbie showed up tonight and directed us to the hidden chapel. Very surprised. Because if her motive was to keep centre stage, then she's blown it away now. She's given up the one hold she had over us: locating Sebastian Banks. Unless. . . .'

Fiona hesitated for a moment. 'Unless she has something else planned. Something guaranteed to keep her centre stage. So have we underestimated Debbie Connelly?'

28

They would never have found the entrance to the cave system without the directions in the script of the mystery play.

Goldilocks had made a series of drawings copied straight from the text and by comparing features in the drawings with the actual landscape, she was able to pinpoint the spot where the knight was gazing across a stream before following it underground. Once that had been established, two officers from the Underwater Rescue Squad launched a Zodiac into the water. The men were wearing wet suits, and one of them started the outboard engine and took the craft across to the other side of the stream. Then the officers began a systematic search of the river-bank which was overgrown with thick patches of bramble, willow and nettle.

Searching the bank was slow work as all the undergrowth had to be hacked away by hand. But in the end they found the opening. It was behind a block of limestone that had slipped at some time in the past and come to rest half in and half out of the water, forcing the stream to twist round it in a swirling eddy.

One of the officers carefully negotiated the eddy and gunned the engine of the Zodiac to keep station in the water as his companion shone a powerful hand-held searchlight behind the rock.

'Zulu to control.' He spoke into the mike attached to his helmet.

'Go ahead, Zulu,' Falcon replied.

'There's an opening at the back of the rock. It's over six foot high, but it veers to the right after a few feet and goes out of sight.'

'Can you get in?'

The officer said something to his companion who worked the

engine and slowly brought the bows of the Zodiac round behind the eddy. For a moment the boat was pushed backwards by the power of the water, but then the bows came into clear water and the officer with the searchlight stepped onto a ledge at the back of the limestone block.

'There's a passage leading into the rock. It ends in a door set into the limestone.'

'OK. Pull back. I'll get an armed response unit to move in.'

On the bank Falcon gestured to one of the men standing in a group of officers. All the men were dressed in full body armour under dark-blue flak jackets. For rapid identification the jackets had a broad strip of material across the back that would fluoresce in the beam of a torch. On their heads they wore baseball caps with POLICE stencilled on them in bright white letters. Five of the officers were carrying Heckler and Koch MP5 submachine-guns, and the sixth had a sniper rifle with a night sight. In addition every member of the team carried pepper spray, tear gas, stun grenades and tasers. The men were linked by a state-of-the-art communication system that Falcon was plugged into via a throat microphone and earphones.

'It's all yours, Dave,' Falcon spoke to the inspector in charge of the unit. 'Keep in contact.'

As they waited, the officer who had entered the cave stepped back into the Zodiac and the craft returned. One of the officers climbed out, but the other kept the outboard running and stayed by the tiller as the six men of the armed response unit climbed aboard. They were an interesting bunch, Fiona thought. Officers who had deliberately chosen to live in that shadow world, halfway between the police and the armed forces. But they were an elite section, highly trained and psychologically tested.

The Zodiac crossed the stream again and the armed unit negotiated the limestone block and entered the narrow passage.

'Alpha One to Control,' The voice of the armed response unit inspector came over the speaker.

'Control, go ahead, Alpha One.' Falcon spoke into his mike.

'Can confirm the passage is empty, but there's some weird stuff on the walls.'

'What kind of stuff?'

'Carvings in the rock. Odd looking beasts and strange symbols.'

'Wait.'

Falcon turned to a man wearing a long brown habit tied at the waist with rope. He was from the community of monks, and was there at Mallory's request to act as liaison between the abbot and the police.

'Brother Jonathan, are these carvings important?'

'Well, their presence would suggest that there's some kind of special place down there.' The monk spoke with a rich deep voice.

'Control to Alpha One. Proceed with extreme caution.'

There was a pause, then the voice came again, 'Alpha One, to control. We've reached the door in the passage. Opening it now.'

Another pause. Longer this time.

'Control, what is it?'

'You'd better see this for yourself, Control. Let my men check the place out, then come in on my all clear.'

'Dave was right. This is weird.' Falcon stopped in the passage and looked at the carvings. 'What are they?'

'They are old. Very old,' Brother Jonathan answered him. 'In early Christianity there were still many pagan images associated with the new religion, and similar carvings are found in some old churches. Here, look at this one.' He pointed to one of the images. 'This is the Earth Mother. And that one.' He pointed to another carving. 'That's the Green Man, a strong pagan image. But they're mixed in with Christian symbols, like the Lamb of God, up there. And the Celtic cross over the arch of the door.'

They moved forward again towards the door where the inspector was waiting. As they approached, he stood back so they could look inside.

'Oh, dear God,' Brother Jonathan whispered the words and raised the crucifix that was hanging around his neck, holding it out in front of him.

Fiona pushed forward so she could see what was on the other side of the door.

It was a chapel carved out of a limestone cavern; wooden

benches in rows in front of a simple altar, below a roof of high arches supported by heavy wooden beams. It was lit now by an array of tall thick candles standing on every surface, the flames flickering in a faint draught and giving the place an ethereal look, an impression heightened by the strong smell of incense hanging on the air.

But these were impressions fleetingly etched on Fiona's consciousness in the second before everything else was driven out by the sight of the figure hanging suspended from the roof above the altar, arms and legs pulled wide apart. The scene had been carefully posed, that was the first thing to cross Fiona's mind. The man wore a crown of thorns on his head, and he was naked except for a loincloth, red now from blood that had flowed from a deep wound in his side. And the final touch; a strip of cardboard had been hung around his neck with the words '*Ecce Homo*' printed on it.

'What does that mean?' Fiona whispered the question.

'*Behold the Man*. The words used by Pontius Pilot when he showed Our Lord Jesus to the crowd on the Via Dolorosa,' Brother Jonathan answered her. Then he crossed himself.

Fiona looked at the face of the man on the steps. And in that instant all her preconceptions were destroyed.

29

'We are dealing with evil here,' Brother Jonathan spoke softly. 'A very great evil.'

Mallory had called the briefing, even though they'd not yet had the preliminary scenes-of-crime report. Because one thing was certain: Brother Jonathan had confirmed the identity of the body to be that of Sebastian Banks. A man he knew well.

The prime suspect in the case was dead.

'A great evil.' Falcon echoed the monk's words 'You mean the killing of Sebastian Banks?'

'The killing, yes. But this is not just a killing. The murdered man wore a crown of thorns and had a spear wound in his side. Make no mistake, this is an enactment of the death of Jesus Christ. And, at the risk of sounding melodramatic, I would say this is the gesture of a tortured soul that has turned to the darkness.'

'Wait a minute,' Goldilocks cut in. 'Can you describe the scene in the chapel, please?'

Falcon ran through the details for her.

'You may well be dealing with a tortured soul here, but from the way you describe the scene it seems to me that whoever did this was following instructions in the mystery play. And I should know, I've been over them enough times.'

'So there was a crucifixion scene in the play?'

'Yes, and part of it was where Pontius Pilate washed his hands of it all. In fact, I remember instructions to hang the notice saying "*Ecce Homo*" around the actor's neck.'

'And can you remember any references to a spear?' Falcon asked.

'Yes, it was mentioned several times in the stage directions.'

'So the killer *was* acting out the mystery play.' Falcon was beginning to sound out of his depth.

Sergeant Maltravers arranged to have Brother Jonathan driven back to the monastery and, when he'd left, Mallory turned to Fiona. 'How does this latest murder affect the investigation?'

'The whole house of cards has collapsed. We all had Sebastian Banks in the frame for the murders, and assumed that he was the ringmaster directing operations. That was the rationale. Now, Sebastian Banks himself has been murdered. Which doesn't prove that he wasn't responsible for the deaths of the three religious leaders, but it does mean that if he was, then there's another killer on the loose. Not impossible, but improbable. Until we get the autopsy report we won't know how long Sebastian Banks has been dead. But the fact that he was killed at all, and especially in a way that mimicked a scene in the mystery play, changes my original thinking and leads to another possible scenario.'

'Go on.' Mallory was watching her closely now.

'My guess is that when Mark heard the two lectures given by Sebastian Banks on recovery from a loss of faith, he saw a chance for his own salvation. A release from everything his bigoted father had put him through for all those years. That was why he stayed close to Banks. So we had two vulnerable people, each trying to rescue their own faith, and probably feeding off each other. And that much still stays the same as it was in my original scenario. But here comes the change. What if sometime around then Mark DeMasters entered what Brother Jonathan called 'the darkness' and once in that state he killed the three religious leaders. And then, the final piece, suppose Sebastian Banks found out that Mark was the murderer and was killed to shut him up.'

'Neat, but it's still just a theory,' Mallory said. 'And in any case, what made DeMasters enter this so-called darkness?'

'As yet, we have no way of knowing that,' Fiona replied. 'But it must have happened after the seminars, otherwise Mark wouldn't have turned to Sebastian Banks for help in the first place. And one thing's for certain, it must have been a very strong trigger event to take him into the darkness. Strong enough to blast away any vestiges of faith Mark had recovered and turn him into a vicious killer who not only killed the religious leaders, but also murdered his friend Sebastian Banks. So in a way, we were right. The religious leaders were killed in an act of frenzy by someone who had lost faith. We just had the wrong man, that's all. Mark DeMasters, not Sebastian Banks, was the ringmaster.'

'It could make sense,' Mallory agreed. 'But unfortunately it's nothing more than pure speculation at the moment. Another house of cards that could just as easily collapse as the first one did.'

'Wait a minute,' Falcon came in. 'I'm not even sure it is a house of cards yet. Let's just pause for a moment and see what we've actually got on DeMasters. The answer is, precious little. We know he had a troubled upbringing. We know he had an inverted cross in his room. We know he met Sebastian Banks. So what? Our case was built on Sebastian Banks being the killer, and Mark DeMasters and Debbie Connelly tagging along, and even that case wasn't exactly brimming over with evidence, was it? In fact, the only real piece of hard evidence that could possibly link Banks to the murders was the monks' robes worn by the killer. Robes that Banks had access to. But then so did Debbie Connelly and for all we know, DeMasters as well. Obviously, we have to change tack now that Sebastian Banks is dead, but we can still tie the original three murders to Sebastian Banks's church in Langley because of the monks' robes. That's a given, but I don't think we can automatically put DeMasters in the frame for the murders. Not without far more substantial evidence anyway.'

Mallory sighed. 'You're right, of course. Fiona's theory is just that. A theory. But we have enough to bring Mark DeMasters in for questioning. So we pull the plug on the manhunt for Sebastian Banks and switch it to DeMasters.'

Mallory was looking for positives to relieve the gloom that was rapidly settling over the investigation. But Falcon was still playing devil's advocate.

'So we switch our attention to DeMasters. For now, at least. But there's another question, isn't there?' He turned to Fiona. 'A question we asked earlier. Where does Debbie Connelly fit into the picture now? She led us to the chapel, but did she know we'd find the body there?'

But Fiona had no answer for him.

30

Mallory opened the next morning's briefing with a question.

'So the only people in the matrix now are Mark DeMasters and Debbie Connelly. Right?'

Fiona agreed. 'Yes, they're our only suspects. But you're right, we still don't know which one is the killer.'

She walked onto the platform and removed the photograph of Sebastain Banks from its circle on the whiteboard, leaving a gaping hole behind.

Falcon gestured towards the two remaining photographs of DeMasters and Debbie Connelly. 'In truth, we still don't have any hard evidence to link either of them directly to the killings.' He sounded depressed.

'No, I agree, we're low on hard evidence,' Fiona agreed.

'And yet again, I put the question: what's Debbie Connelly's role in all this?' Falcon asked.

'We don't know for sure that she does have a role,' Fiona replied. 'But setting up the murders required a great deal of organization, and we know Debbie was an insider as far as the mystery play was concerned. In other words, she was in a position to get hold of the murder weapons, and even to reshape the play to her own needs. But the problem is, we still can't actually link her to Mark DeMasters. Not unless scenes-of-crime can find evidence to show they were both in the chapel. But what about the photo of Mark DeMasters that was shown around the village? Anything there?'

'A number of people remembered seeing him, but nobody ever

saw him with Debbie Connelly. And even if we do link the two of them, what then?' Falcon pushed the point.

'I'm not certain. We know Debbie's an attention seeker. To the extent that she effectively fingered Sebastian Banks as the God Slayer by citing the robes which she said no one else knew about. Then she told us about the vicar's sanctuary, and she stayed in the limelight while she led the search for it. At that stage, she was in control of things. But then Goldilocks threatened to pull the plug on the search, and Debbie had no choice then. She had to deliver or we'd drop her. So deliver she did. She showed us the way to the chapel. But we don't know if she had anything to do with what we found there. So have we finished with her? I just don't know. But I very much doubt it.'

'So now we concentrate on finding Mark DeMasters himself. Do you want the media brought in to start another manhunt at this stage, guv?'

'I think so. We'll give out details, or at least some details, on the murder in the chapel. And we'll say that Sebastian Banks is dead and the search has switched to Mark DeMasters. If nothing else, it will show the public that our investigation's moving along. So I'll get on to the press office.'

'Speaking of the media, what about last night's TV programme?' Falcon put the question.

'What TV programme?' Fiona asked.

'So you didn't watch the Northern Vista last night?'

'No, I went back to the Special Hospital to catch up on a couple of things. It was late when I got back, and I didn't have the TV on at all.'

'Apparently, a TV reporter had got hold of the story that a group of orthodox Jews had come over from the States in search of a great secret hidden somewhere in the James Street synagogue. The reporter didn't know what the secret was, but she said there were rumours that it enabled the holder to speak directly to God. And the idea was made all the more intriguing by the fact that no one from the synagogue agreed to give interviews.'

'This is just the kind of story the national media will pick up.' Falcon said. 'So I think we can expect the James Street area to be inundated by reporters.'

'I agree,' Mallory nodded. 'But what I'm really concerned about is all the publicity this will generate. Sooner or later, some bright spark is going to make the quite erroneous assumption that there's a connection between the secret artefact, the murders of the religious leaders, and the Faith Conference. Bloody hell, half of the world's media will be in Garton for a story like that.'

Before Mallory could continue, one of the detectives working the investigation came to the table and spoke to Falcon.

'There's a call for you from a Dr Perdue at the university. He says it's important. Shall I route it through to here?'

'Go ahead.'

The detective left and a a few moments later one of the phones on the table rang out.

Falcon lifted the receiver and identified himself. Then he listened to the message, thanked the caller and replaced the receiver.

'There's been a robbery at Dr Perdue's office when he was at a meeting. As far as he can tell there was only one item taken.'

'And what was that?' Mallory asked.

'An undergraduate thesis written by Mark DeMasters.'

'What was the title of this thesis?' Fiona asked.

'*A Study of Religious Symbolism in the Architecture of Garton.*'

31

'Are you sure nothing else was taken?' Falcon asked.

The three of them, Dr Perdue, Falcon and Fiona were sitting in the departmental coffee room as a scenes-of-crime unit checked out Perdue's office.

'Not as far as I can tell, no. When I came back from my meeting I found a small pane of glass in the door had been smashed and the door itself was open. But when I looked around, nothing seemed to have been disturbed. But there had been a break-in, that much was obvious, so I made a careful search and it was then I noticed that the thesis had gone.'

'What kind of theses are these?' Fiona asked.

'They're written by undergraduates as part of the final exams. Each student is assigned a supervisor who helps with the research needed and oversees the presentation. I was Mark's supervisor, and the thesis was in my room prior to being marked by two assessors. It was kept on a shelf with the other theses I'd supervised.'

'We know the title of the thesis, but what exactly is it about?'

'The idea behind it was to look for special kinds of symbols in the religious buildings in the city. Carvings in stone, stained-glass windows, statues. That kind of thing.'

'OK.' Falcon moved the questioning forward. 'What else can you tell us about the thesis?'

'I can only give you a general outline because I hadn't read it fully before it was stolen. I can tell you that I directed Mark to look first for any kind of pagan symbols that had carried over into Christian churches. Then I suggested that he look at symbolism in the synagogues, and it was at that stage that the thesis really took off.'

'In what way?'

'As part of his survey he spoke to the rabbi at the James Street synagogue. Apparently, there's a myth associated with the synagogue. Something to do with a treasure brought out of Israel at the fall of Solomon's temple. It was guarded by a Jewish sect in Prague and was eventually brought to Garton during WWII. But it was lost, or maybe deliberately hidden away, and no one knows where it is now. Mark became fascinated by the story.'

'How far did he get with his research?'

'That's the strange thing. I got the distinct impression that he found out more than he put into the thesis.'

'But why should Mark DeMasters want to steal a copy of his own thesis?' Fiona asked.

'It must have contained something that he wanted to keep from other people,' Dr Perdue replied. 'Something he only realized the importance of after he'd submitted the work.'

'But you hadn't read the thesis yourself?'

'No, it was still on my list of jobs to do. But Chris Barfoot has read it.'

'So Dr Perdue told you that Mark DeMasters had become interested in the secret that's associated with the James Street synagogue,' Mallory said.

They were back in the major operations room, sitting at the long table drinking coffee.

'Yes, it looks that way,' Fiona answered. 'But we don't know what was in the thesis, and Dr Perdue can't tell us because he hadn't got around to reading it. But let's see if we can fit everything to a time line.'

She walked over to the whiteboard that still displayed the photographs of Debbie Connelly and Mark DeMasters, and picked up a marker pen.

'The thesis was written over the first and second semesters of the final year; say October 2008 to March 2009.'

She wrote that on the board.

'The *Belief in Crisis* seminars were held when?'

'I'll check with the university.' Goldilocks went away and returned a few minutes later.

'They were held over the week of the 23rd to the 27th March.'

Fiona added the info to the board.

'And the first killing, the rabbi?'

'April the sixth.' Falcon said.

That too was added to the board.

'Then the murders of the other two religious leaders, were when?'

'The seventh and eighth of April.'

'And finally, the date of the murder of Sebastian Banks - which we don't know yet.'

She arranged the dates she had in a linear sequence at the base of the board.

'So if we assume for the moment that Mark DeMasters did kill Sebastian Banks, then there are two vital pieces of data we need before we can see if the times fit any kind of pattern. The first is the date Sebastian Banks was killed, and the second is the date of the trigger event I identified earlier. The event that sent Mark DeMasters into the darkness.'

'In your new scenario you're assuming that DeMasters murdered Sebastian Banks. Are you also assuming that DeMasters, and not Banks, murdered the three religious leaders?'

'It would seem realistic for now, yes. And not just because Mark's the only game in town. He goes a long way to fitting the profile of the killer. True, so did Sebastian Banks at one time. But concentrate on Mark for a moment. One, in his entire life he's been in what you might call a crisis of faith as a result of his weird upbringing at the hands of his father. Two, he apparently suffered some kind of trauma that flipped him into the darkness. And three, the clincher for me, is the inverted cross in his room, because that shows the extent to which he's turned against religion now. That, and the way the murder in the chapel was staged. So, of the two people left in the matrix, I believe we know now which is the killer: Mark DeMasters.'

Before Falcon could answer Goldilocks called to him. Falcon had asked her to check the CCTV images from around the James Street synagogue and she was standing by a detective at one of the work stations on the main floor area.

'I think you should see this, guv.'

Falcon and Fiona crossed to the work station where Goldilocks was leaning over the shoulder of the detective.

'What is it?' Falcon asked.

'This is from one of the cameras just up the street from the synagogue, and I've frozen a frame for you. Look.' She moved away, so the others could see the screen. 'The camera's covering the steps leading to the house where the Guardians are staying. And see who's just about to approach the front door.'

'Well, well. Debbie Connelly.' Falcon murmured. 'What the hell's she playing at?'

32

'This is a whole new ball game.' Falcon said.

They were back around the table and Logan had joined them.

'When was the CCTV footage taken?' Fiona asked Goldilocks.

'At five minutes past ten today. The cameras are checked every two hours. Five minutes earlier and this footage would have been reviewed two hours ago. As it is, she's probably long gone now. But here.' She passed Mallory a glossy coloured photo. 'I had this run off.'

'Thanks.' Mallory placed the photo on the table. 'OK, lets get Aaron Levi over here. No time for kid gloves now.' Mallory was thinking on his feet, spurred on by the new evidence. 'And once we've talked to Aaron Levi we'll pay the Guardians a visit. We need them to tell us why Debbie Connelly went to see them.' He turned to Goldilocks. 'Can you please arrange to pick up Aaron Levi? I'd rather he came voluntarily, but if he argues, bring him in under caution. But I don't think that will be necessary. So be nice to him. Use all your charm, because I want him on side.'

'That sounds almost sexist, sir.'

'Damned right it is.'

'Oh, well, anything for the force, I suppose.' She flounced off with an exaggerated hip-swinging walk.

'Right.' With an effort Mallory stopped watching Goldilocks disappear, and turned to Falcon.

'Why should Debbie Connelly contact the Guardians?'

'A thought.' It was Fiona who answered. 'It's my guess that she still wants to be centre stage. So maybe she has something that the

Guardians need. Something that will put her back in the limelight.'

Falcon suddenly snapped his fingers. 'The thesis. Maybe DeMasters broke into Dr Perdue's office and took his own thesis to show to Debbie Connelly because there was something in it that relates to this secret artefact the Guardians are looking for.'

'That would make sense,' Mallory agreed. 'But remember, we still can't prove that she ever met Mark DeMasters.'

They took a coffee break at that stage and, as they finished, Goldilocks came back bringing Aaron Levi with her.

'Thank you for coming.' Mallory shook his hand.

Aaron Levi grinned mischievously. 'How could I refuse such a messenger?'

He seemed relaxed, Fiona thought. So maybe Dan Logan had been wrong to suspect Aaron Levi's judgement might be coloured by the presence of the Guardians at his synagogue.

'So how can I help, Assistant Chief Constable.'

'There are some questions we'd like to ask you about the so-called Guardians that are currently visiting your synagogue.'

'Ah, so you know about them? It's the TV programme last night, I suppose?'

'No, we've known about them for some time now.' Mallory didn't elaborate on that. 'But we were intrigued by the item on TV. Apparently, the reporter fronting the programme said that a secret artefact that was somehow connected to a way of speaking directly to God, was hidden somewhere in the James Street synagogue. Do you believe this? About speaking directly to God, I mean?'

But Aaron Levi wouldn't be drawn on the subject. 'It is perhaps enough that the members of the sect in the States believe it. And take my word, this sect isn't on its own in believing that some lost secret has been assigned to their care. History's full of sects guarding the Holy Grail, or the Ark of the Covenant, or the location of the tomb of Jesus.'

'All right, I accept that.' Mallory didn't want to go too far down that road. 'Have the Guardians tried to locate the artefact before?'

'Oh, yes, there have been several detailed searches of the synagogue since the end of the war, but all without success.'

'So why are they here now?' Falcon asked.

'As soon as they learned the rabbi had been murdered they were afraid it might be connected in some way to the artefact. In the end, of course, the murders of the other two religious leaders meant that the synagogue wasn't the centre of all the activity. But then the TV programme was broadcast and everything became public.'

'So where do we stand with the sect now?' Mallory asked.

'They were disturbed by the item on TV because they believe that all sorts of lunatics will come out of the woodwork and start looking for the location of the artefact. So, right now, they're even more desperate than ever to find it themselves before anyone else does.'

'OK.' Mallory clearly wanted to move on. 'Let me ask a practical question.' He pushed the CCTV photograph across the table. 'Have you seen this woman before?'

Aaron Levi studied the photograph. 'Yes, she's from the Faith Conference office. Her name's Debbie Connelly. She came to see me this morning. Do you know her?'

'Oh, yes, we know her.'

33

'Had you met Debbie Connelly before?' Mallory asked.

'No.'

'Did you ask for identification?'

'Yes, of course I did. We've been very conscious of security ever since the murder of the rabbi. As you well know.'

'So what kind of ID did she have?' Falcon asked.

'One of those plastic cards that hang around the neck.'

'And what was on it?'

'Standard information. The Faith Conference logo, the woman's name, a pass number and a colour photograph. Why, is there something wrong?'

Mallory nodded. 'There could very well be. Debbie Connelly has been helping us with our inquiries for some time now. But, there's no way she works for the Faith Conference office.'

'OK, let's look at the question of the ID first.' Falcon turned to Goldilocks. 'Can you contact the Faith Conference office, please? Check out if Connelly was issued with a security pass, and if so why?'

She left the room and Falcon switched back to Aaron Levi.

'So Debbie Connelly pretended to be from the Faith Conference. But why? What did she want?'

'She said she'd seen the item about the artefact on the local TV news, and knew about the Guardians, as you call them, from the programme. And she wanted to talk to them.'

'What about?'

'She said it was something to do with the opening ceremony of the Faith Conference.'

'So what did you do?'

'I told her I had no authority to speak for the sect, but that I would be glad to arrange for her to meet them.'

'She definitely implied that she was representing the Faith Conference?'

'Yes, she did, yes. And I saw no reason to doubt it having seen her identification badge. Now, of course, I know she wasn't from the Faith Conference. So why should she say she was? I don't understand.'

'I think I do,' Fiona said. 'It was simply a way of getting you to listen to her. Without the identification, would you have let her within miles of the Guardians?'

'No, I suppose not.'

'But as it was, you led her to them.'

'Yes. I had to attend an important meeting, but I phoned the house where the sect members are staying. When they agreed to see Miss Connelly, I showed her where the house was and she went there alone. The place is very close, otherwise I would have got someone to take her over there.'

'And that must have been when she was caught on CCTV.' Falcon said. 'So what happened at the meeting between Debbie Connelly and the Guardians, do you know?'

'No, I'm afraid not. Once I got back from the meeting I was attending I had a full schedule. I intended to follow up on Miss Connelly's visit, but I hadn't got around to it before you asked me to come here.'

'We have to assume, as Gary suggested earlier, that whatever it was that Debbie Connelly could offer the sect was contained in the stolen thesis. So we have to get onto them soonest and since they might be suspicious of the police, I'd like you to act as liaison, Mr Levi.'

'Of course. I'll do everything I can to—' He paused as Sergeant Maltravers came back.

'I've found out about the ID. It was issued to Debbie Connelly as the assistant to Sebastian Banks when they were rehearsing the mystery play. It's to be staged in the street between the two cathedrals as part of the opening ceremony, and apparently Debbie needed access to various places, such as storage rooms, which is why she was issued with the pass.'

'So, it's genuine?' Falcon asked.

'Absolutely,' Goldilocks agreed. 'And unless we block it, it'll get her into all the sites associated with the Faith Conference.'

Mallory nodded. But he was more worried about why a thesis written by an undergraduate student should be of interest to the sect.

34

'You guys want coffee?' The question was asked in a strong American accent.

Falcon and Fiona were standing with Aaron Levi in a long room at the rear of the house where the Guardians were staying. The room was dominated by a long dark-oak trestle table that was covered in architectural drawings, yellow notepads, empty styrene coffee cups and cartons of doughnuts.

Not very different from the table in the major incident room, Fiona thought. Except the way the six people standing round it were dressed. Long black coats, white shirts and black hats. Like uniforms.

The man who had asked about coffee came round the table with cups on a metal tray. He handed the cups out to the visitors, then moved to the head of the table. 'OK, Mr Levi said the police wanted to talk to us, and I'd like to make one thing very clear from the start.'

'Go ahead.' Falcon was non-committal.

'We belong to a sect in America that believes its members are the guardians of a secret that was first passed on to them at the fall of Solomon's Temple.'

'We know about the sect,' Falcon cut in. 'And we know about its ties to the James Street synagogue here in Garton?'

'That's good, because it will save a lot of explanations. But the point I want to make clear is that our only concern is to safeguard the secret, and I want to stress we will not interfere in any investigation run by the local cops. In fact, we will be only to happy to be of any help we can.'

'Thank you. I appreciate that.' Falcon was obviously prepared to take a softly-softly approach once the boundaries were clear. At least for the time being.

'So what is this secret?'

'I'm sorry, but I can't tell you, and no outside pressure, or come to that court orders, will change our line. But, from what we learned after we came over here, I think we can assume that the secret played no part in the murder of the rabbi.'

'Because?' Falcon was still happy to probe. To find out how much the sect knew.

'Because of the other two murders. Both involved the leaders of different religions. Whoever the killer is, he's some oddball who hates religion. *All* religion. Not someone who's after an ancient secret entrusted to the care of an obscure Jewish sect.'

'So why stay around once you knew that?' Fiona saw it then. Falcon was leading him into a corner. 'Because it's my understanding that you don't know the location of the secret artefact.'

The man looked at Falcon, as if he was trying to read his mind. Then he shrugged. 'We don't know the exact location of the artefact, true. It was lost during WWII. But we know it was hidden somewhere in the area of the synagogue. And while we're over here we plan to find it. That's what all that's about.' He indicated the material on the table. 'We're trying to run down the location.'

Falcon nodded, apparently satisfied with the explanation. 'So how close are you to finding it?'

The man shrugged again, and offered a wry smile. 'We're no closer than we were when we came here.'

'Not even with what Debbie Connelly was able to tell you?'

There. The trap was sprung now.

The silence seemed to drag out and Falcon made no attempt to end it, content to leave that to the Guardians.

'OK, so you know about Debbie Connelly. And yeah, she did say she could help us locate the artefact.'

'How come she was in a position to help?' Falcon was trying to find out how much they would tell him.

'She'd seen the piece about us on local TV, and told us her boyfriend had written a thesis on religious architecture in the city. As part of that he'd studied the James Street synagogue, and she thought he'd stumbled on the location of the secret that was mentioned in the TV programme. But when she was asked if she'd been to the location herself she'd said no because there was a risk in approaching it openly. And she said she wouldn't reveal the location to us. Not without strings attached anyway.'

So they'd been right, Fiona thought. Debbie Connelly had been prepared to offer them the thing they wanted most of all: the location of the artefact.

'So what was she offering you?' Falcon asked.

'The information in the thesis.'

'In exchange for what?'

The silence was drawn out again.

'In exchange for what?' Falcon repeated the question.

'For us agreeing to display it at the opening ceremony of the conference. In her presence, so she's a part of it.'

'Centre stage,' Fiona said the words softly.

'Does that make sense?' Falcon asked her.

'Oh, yes. It makes perfect sense. She made sure she was centre stage when she told us about the play and then led us to the chapel. But that's all redundant now, so she probably had something else lined up to stay centre stage. But she seems to have dropped that as well when she learned about the sect. And think about it. What better way to keep in the limelight than being associated with revelation of the lost artefact at the opening ceremony of the Faith Conference? An artefact that allows people to talk directly to God.'

'And you agreed to this?' Falcon sounded surprised.

He shrugged. 'Our top priority is to locate the artefact. Nothing else even comes close. And if recovering it means that we have to put it on display for a while, then so be it. It's a price we're prepared to pay.'

Falcon nodded. 'So Debbie will give you the location of the artefact in exchange for the world learning of the part she played in finding it. And to reinforce that she'll take part in a modified

140

opening ceremony of the Faith Conference?'

'Yes.'

'But the organizers of the conference will have to agree to that, won't they?'

'Sure. But we figure they'll bend over backwards to show the artefact as part of their celebrations.'

'Yes, I can see that.' Falcon said. 'But there's a flaw in all this, isn't there? Once you've located the artefact what's to stop you just dumping Debbie Connelly?'

'She intends to approach the TV reporter who ran the original story and offer her an exclusive on the latest developments. All of them, including our involvement. That way, her position is safeguarded if we renege on any agreement, as she will still be associated with the story of the artefact the reporter puts on TV. But in any case, as long as the artefact is not in danger, we fully expect to keep our side of the bargain.'

'And do you have an agreement?'

'We're moving towards one, yes. Debbie Connelly is returning here this evening. And she will bring her boyfriend's thesis with her.'

Falcon finished briefing Mallory on the visit to the Guardians.

'So Debbie Connelly has finally broken away from us now she has bigger fish to fry. But we can spring a trap and arrest her when she returns to the house,' Mallory said. 'Except, of course, Debbie Connelly isn't our number one priority. That's DeMasters. So, now we've been given an opportunity to locate Debbie Connelly I suggest we continue giving her a free rein. Let her work with the sect, but follow her when she leaves. We can set that up with Dan Logan.'

He paused as Goldilocks came onto the dais. She was grinning like the Chesire Cat.

'I think I've found the trigger that turned Mark DeMasters into a killer.'

35

Goldilocks faced her audience.

'I started to dig around a bit to put some flesh on the bones of what Dr Perdue had told us about Mark DeMasters. First, I got Mark's home address from the university and contacted the local police. They knew the name, and put me onto Social Services.'

She paused to consult her notebook. 'As an organization Social Services are, quite rightly, reluctant to open their records to other services, and in any case they don't always see eye to eye with the police. So I got the ACC to arrange for a court order as back-up for when I talked to them. But, as it turned out, when they learned we were conducting a murder inquiry they were fully co-operative, and put me onto the case worker who'd dealt with the family.

'Mark had a sister, Isabel, who was a year younger than him, and it seems that the family had been known to Social Services for around five years. The services first came in contact with Mark's parents following a formal complaint by one of Isabel's teachers. Apparently, Isabel had just started at secondary school and, when she was in the changing room the teacher noticed she had heavy bruising on various parts of her body. She reported it to the head, who passed it on to Social Services.

'Once they were made aware of the bruising on Isabel's body, they undertook an enquiry, but apparently Isabel herself said the bruises resulted from a fall down the stairs. The case worker carrying out the enquiry didn't believe her but, as in many cases like this, she couldn't prove anything. She did, however, carry out a full home circumstances investigation. It turned up some odd behaviour in the family dynamics, and it supported what Mark later told Dr Perdue about the father being a religious bigot who brought his children up according to a strict religious code. Apparently the mother was weak, and rarely stood up to him. Under those circumstances Mark and Isabel joined forces, and it seems Mark was ultra-protective towards his younger sister. But the case worker made no mention of any hidden punishment room, and in the end it was decided to take no action, but to keep the family under review.'

'And did they have cause to take action later?' Fiona asked.

'No, they had no evidence to do so. But the case worker told me that when the time came for Mark to go to university he was worried about his sister and stayed at home for another year until she'd finished school. She'd planned to go to university herself, and although it wasn't here in Garton, Mark felt she'd be safe enough on her own providing she was away from her father. But it seems he was wrong.'

'In what way?' Fiona asked.

'When the involvement of the Social Services ended, the case worker lost track of them both, until July this year when she read a piece in the local newspaper about the death of a student in London. That student was Isabel DeMasters and, according to the reporter, her death had been particularly tragic. She'd been a bright girl who was expected to get a first class honours degree. But during the last year she'd fallen in with the wrong crowd and had moved onto the drug scene. Apparently her father found out. He was in London on some private business and decided to visit Isabel. But when he went to her address he was told she hadn't lived there for months. One of the students gave him another address for Isabel, and when he got there he found his daughter was a druggy living in a squat with a crowd of other users. Witnesses in the squat said her father ranted and raved at Isabel, screaming that she was a daughter of Satan, and that he never wanted to see her again. The next day she took her own life. When the coroner at the inquest into Isabel's death heard evidence from other people living in the squat he expressed the view that had her father been more sympathetic there may have been a chance for her to get her life back on track.'

'And Mark DeMasters found out what had happened?' Fiona asked.

'Yes. Isabel had a boyfriend at the squat. He knew about Mark and he phoned him the day Isabel killed herself. He told Mark about all the things his father had said, and that in his opinion that was why Isabel had killed herself.'

'You were right.' Fiona turned to Goldilocks. 'You've identified the trigger event that turned Mark DeMasters. Good work.'

'Why, thank you. Perhaps you should put it on my record. It might persuade some people I'm worthy of promotion.' She rolled her eyes in an exaggerated fashion.

Falcon grinned, but didn't pursue the topic. 'So how does identifying the trigger event help us find DeMasters?' He put the question to Fiona.

'I'm not sure it does yet,' she replied. 'But we did pick up one vital piece of evidence from talking to the sect. Debbie Connelly told them her boyfriend had written a thesis on religious architecture in the city. Her *boyfriend*. And we know that the thesis was written by Mark DeMasters. So at last, we're able to positively link Debbie and Mark on the basis of hard evidence.'

'And with Sebastian Banks dead, there are only two people in the matrix now: Debbie Connelly, a drama queen seeking attention, and Mark DeMasters, a very disturbed personality seeking revenge.'

'Attention and revenge.' Fiona sounded worried. 'That could make a lethal combination.'

Before she could elaborate, Falcon's mobile rang. After he'd taken the call he turned to the others. 'That was Dan Logan. Bad news, I'm afraid. Debbie Connelly failed to make the meeting with the Americans.'

The bag lady stood in the shadows of a narrow alley opposite the house where the sect members were staying.

For a moment she swayed slightly on her feet and steadied herself against the wall before taking a drink out of the bottle she carried wrapped in brown paper. A typical wino. Except for her eyes, which were sharp and clear as she scanned the steps leading up to the house.

She was patient, prepared to wait. And that patience was rewarded when she saw a man enter the house. A man she'd first seen talking to Goldilocks at police HQ.

So the Guardians had betrayed her. Time to turn to the TV people.

36

'No sign of Debbie Connelly yet?' Falcon asked Aaron Levi as Goldilocks brought him to the major operations room.

'No, I think we have to accept the fact that she's not coming back.'

'Are we sure she's not just late?' Fiona asked.

'It's possible, I suppose. But she should have shown over an hour ago.'

'So why do you think she failed to turn up?'

Aaron Levi shrugged. 'I don't know, I'm afraid. But the Americans think she might have made her own deal with the TV people, a deal that would keep them out in the cold.'

'That could make sense,' Fiona said. 'What better way could she have of staying centre stage than being in front of the massive media coverage around the Faith Conference. Especially if the artefact is displayed.'

Falcon turned to Goldilocks. 'Can you get Cathleen Forster from the press office to join us. We need her input if the TV people are involved.'

A few minutes later Goldilocks came back bringing the director of communications with her. Cathleen Forster was in her late twenties. Her blonde hair was short and the features of her face were strong, giving her a no-nonsense air, an impression reinforced by the severely cut dark business suit she was wearing.

'You wanted to see me, Gary?'

'Yes, thanks for coming. I need your input because we might just have a problem with TV coverage.' Quickly he brought her up to speed on the investigation.

'So we think Connelly may try, or indeed even already have tried, to strike a deal with the media. So how would a TV company react if she told them she'd located the secret artefact, and offered them an exclusive on how she plans to reveal it to the world?'

'You've got to be joking. It would be the scoop of the year, maybe even the decade.'

'So, bottom line. Debbie Connelly would have her centre stage role in spades, and the TV company wouldn't come running to us with the details of what she intended to do, even though they know we're in the middle of a murder investigation?'

'Absolutely not. They'd claim that they were unaware of any connection between the artefact and the murders.'

'Right.' Mallory was quiet for a moment. 'Cathy, can you feel out the mood among the media people? Concentrate on the reporter who ran the piece on local TV. It'll be difficult to get them to reveal anything, I know, but someone might let the odd detail slip.'

'I'll try, although with a scoop of this kind, it's my guess security will be tight. But I suppose I could play the divide and rule approach. Let the rumour out that we know some reporter has stumbled on an earth shattering revelation. That might just set the cat among the pigeons. One thing you can say about reporters is that they don't like being scooped by other reporters. So, I'll see what I can turn up.'

When she'd gone, Mallory began to pace up and down. It was a habit of his when he was thinking, and the others didn't interrupt him. When he finally stopped he turned to Falcon.

'How long is it to the opening ceremony?'

'It's scheduled for noon this Sunday, two days from now.'

'So until then Debbie Connelly has to stay in hiding. She told the Guardians that she knew where the artefact was, but she said she hadn't retrieved it at the time because there was a risk in approaching the hiding place openly. So, either Debbie Connelly or Mark DeMasters, or both of them, has to break cover and come out into the open to collect the artefact some time before noon Sunday. If we could locate it before them, we can spring a trap and catch the prey. Both of them, with any luck.'

Mallory sounded as if he relished the thought.

37

'What exactly happened to the treasure after it had been brought to Garton?' Mallory asked Goldilocks, who'd got one of her team to put together a report on the events at the time.

Goldilocks consulted her notebook.

'One night there was a particularly intense air raid, and the area around the synagogue was badly damaged, with half the buildings destroyed and fires raging. Apparently, it got so bad at one time that the two Guardians decided to evacuate the artefact to place of greater safety. There were some eye-witness accounts from that time, but all that could be established with any certainty was that the Guardians left the building around half past one, and were found by an air raid warden at seven the next morning under the ruins of a house that had taken a direct hit. But there was no sign of the artefact, and it was always assumed that they'd hidden it in the synagogue and then left the building themselves. When you consider it that would make sense if they'd found a secure hiding place for it that could withstand the synagogue collapsing but that for some reason, say size, was not safe for people to shelter in. So, they would have exited the building, intending to return for the artefact when it was safe to do so. But they didn't return, of course, because they were both killed in the bombing raid.'

'Let's think about this for a minute.' Falcon turned to Aaron Levi. 'You said once that several searches had been made in an effort to locate the artifact?'

'Over the years, yes.'

'How detailed were the searches.'

'One particular search was very detailed indeed. It was funded by a rich American benefactor and used state of the art technology.'

'OK, we know the Guardians left the synagogue because their bodies were found in the bombed-out house, but they didn't have the artefact with them. Up to now, it's been assumed that they found a place of safety and left the artefact behind in the synagogue. A place they could get back to even if the synagogue was destroyed in the bombing, as apparently seemed likely at the time. But let's assume for the moment that they took the artefact with them when they left the synagogue. What would have been their chief objective in doing that?'

'The safety of the artefact,' Aaron Levi replied.

'Then let's look at the area around the James Street synagogue, see if we can identify any potential sites where it might have been hidden. Sergeant, can you pull up a map of the area for us?'

'I'm on to it.' Goldilocks crossed the platform and the others followed her as she sat down at one of the computers.

Falcon turned to Aaron Levi. 'I accept that you don't know what the artefact is, but do you have any idea of the size of it?'

'Yes, we do. According to the rabbi at the time, when the two Guardians appeared they had in their possession a narrow ornate wooden box about two feet long and six inches wide.'

'Small enough to be carried around?'

'Yes, and there was no indication that it was especially heavy.'

'So what would the Guardians have been looking for if they did bring it out of the synagogue that night?'

'Somewhere safe,' Aaron Levi said.

'Remember they were in the middle of an air raid,' Falcon came in again. 'So what would constitute a place of safety?'

'Somewhere in the open,' Aaron Levi replied. 'If the area was in flames and buildings were coming down, as we know they were on that night, the Guardians wouldn't just simply find another building and swap one danger for another. They'd want to be outside, as far away as they could from falling debris.'

'Let's see what we've got.' Falcon stood behind Goldilocks who'd brought up a map of the area around James Street.

'We've got a problem here, of course.' Aaron Levi shook his head. 'This is a map of the area today, and there's been a tremendous amount of reconstruction following the war damage. Don't we have access to older maps?'

'We might be able to get to them via some of the search engines,' Goldilocks replied. 'But there is another way.'

'And what's that?' Falcon asked.

'There's an archivist working in the museum who specializes in reconstructing original scenes from old photographs and maps. She has some very sophisticated computer programmes. I worked with her once when she was helping me to set-up our facial recognition software. I'm sure she can reconstruct the James Street area during the Forties. Especially if we have old photographs for her to work from.'

'No problem,' Aaron Levi said. 'We have our own archives at the synagogue, and we could provide your friend with masses of photographic material.'

'Right, the programme's loaded, so let's see what we can do.' Candice Frost started to scan a series of old photographs and maps into the computer. She was young, mid-twenties, and casually dressed in jeans and a blue sweatshirt with *Garton Gladiators* emblazoned across it.

Falcon had suggested that it would be quicker if they used police headquarters as a work station. That way, Candice Frost could bring her software and Aaron Levi could bring his material to a central place.

After Falcon had explained what they wanted, Candice had sifted through the pile of material Aaron Levi had brought from the synagogue, rejecting most of it and leaving a much smaller pile of maps and photographs behind. When they'd all been scanned into the computer, Candice spent the next few minutes tapping keys in a rapid succession that coalesced into a blur for the watchers.

'First off, here's a reconstruction of the area around the synagogue

151

as it would have been in the 1940s before most of the bombing occurred. I can't be more accurate for a time frame because the pics span the whole decade. As you asked, I've concentrated at first on how the area would look to someone standing at the entrance to the synagogue.'

Slowly a picture began to scroll down the screen.

'The image can be projected in various forms, but as the material I was given is in black and white, it will come up with a slight sepia touch just because that adds a bit of flavour to old scenes.'

As more of the image was revealed, Fiona felt she was looking out of a window into the past.

In places the image was indistinct, where Candice had used the old maps to landscape the view, and in others it was quite sharp where photos had been inputted to the computer. Finally, the screen was full, and they could see the simulation of the area around the synagogue as if they were there themselves.

'Wow, I'm impressed.' Aaron Levi broke the silence. 'There have been a lot of changes since the Forties. For one thing, you could see right down to the river from the entrance to the synagogue then. Now it's all built up, and there's an industrial park where there used to be open ground.'

But in the simulation one feature dominated the screen. It lay at the far side of the open ground: a structure that was completely hidden now, but would have been clearly seen by anyone leaving the synagogue in the 1940s air raids.

A tall, narrow pyramid.

'What's that?' Fiona pointed to the pyramid.

'I think its some kind of war memorial,' Candice Frost said. 'Hang on a minute, and I'll pull it up on the museum website. Is there another computer I can use, so we can keep the simulation on the screen.'

'Sure.' Goldilocks led her over to a vacant computer, switched it on and typed in a password.

Candice Frost sat in front of the screen and brought up the Garton Museum website. Then as she keyed *sphinx war memorial* into the search facility a photograph of a tall pyramid unrolled on the screen, and she began to read from the text under it.

'*This war memorial, which is dedicated to the 1st Battalion of the Royal Garton Fusiliers, was funded by public subscription in 1805 in recognition of the part played by the Battalion in the battle of Alexandria in 1801. For their service in Egypt the Battalion was allowed to incorporate a pyramid, and the date 1801, into their cap badges.*

'*The Pyramid War Memorial, which bears the names of the men killed in the Egyptian campaign, was sited in a prominent spot in the graveyard of an old church, by the side of the main dock thoroughfare. But the church was in a bad state of repair and it was demolished in 1952, and the area is now predominantly industrial. The memorial is built on a flagged area enclosed by a low chain fence and is maintained by the Royal Garton Fusiliers Society. On more than one occasion it has been proposed that the memorial be moved to a more suitable site. However, to date, nothing has come of this.*'

'Thank you.' Falcon nodded to Candice Frost. 'So, according to the simulation the pyramid would have been clearly visible from the synagogue in the 1940s. It's just possible the two men decided to use that for the safe-keeping of the artefact, and that Debbie Connelly discovered it from something in Mark DeMaster's thesis. Of course, we don't know what's in the thesis, but it's about old religious buildings in Garton, and the war memorial was placed in the graveyard of a church that was demolished. Maybe, DeMasters visited the site and found something that made him believe the pyramid was involved in the storage of the lost artefact. Something Debbie picked up on later. And if that's right it would have made sense to leave the artefact where it was until she needed it because approaching the pyramid in daylight would have carried a risk on that busy road.'

'Sounds plausible,' Aaron Levi agreed.

'The first thing we have to do is check the pyramid to see if the artefact is actually there. And this is where the Guardians can help because if we take them to the pyramid they can identify anything we find there.'

Falcon turned to Aaron Levi. 'Do you think they'll agree to that?'

'Agree to it? After all these years they'll leap at the idea if they think it will lead to the artifact's recovery. I can absolutely guarantee their full co-operation.'

'And if it is there, we surround the area and let the mice walk into the trap. Just as we'd hoped.'

38

It had been a long day. Very long, Fiona thought as the party, including Aaron Levi and two Americans, left the unmarked police van and approached the war memorial from the Dock Road.

The memorial was still cut off by the low chain fence, but on three sides it was now surrounded by steel panels topped with razor wire to protect the industrial park beyond. As the light began to fade the bulk of the pyramid cast a deep shadow, leaving the flagged expanse around it in darkness.

The pyramid itself was constructed of red sandstone blocks, and Falcon walked to the front and shone a torch onto the face. An arch, made up of two vertical pillars supporting a lintel, was set against the outside of the pyramid. A circle was cut into the lintel with the image of a sphinx inside it. On the face of the pyramid carved into the stone above the arch the inscription read:

1st *Battalion, the Royal Garton Fusiliers.*
The Battle of Alexandria in 1801

Below, the names of the men killed in the battle were listed.

'So put yourself in the shoes of the two Guardians on the night of the bombing,' Falcon said. 'They were on unfamiliar ground in the middle of a massive air raid and they were carrying the artefact with them. Then they approach the pyramid. Perhaps they thought it might offer a place of safety to hide the artefact, but only, and this is important, if it had easy access. Because unless they left the synagogue carrying tools with them they would have had no means of breaking into it. Which means that if they did use the pyramid, the way in must have been easy.'

'And obvious,' said Fiona. 'Because with the raid on they wouldn't have had much time.'

'Then I think we could be on a wild goose chase.' Falcon suddenly sounded tired. 'The only way of getting into the pyramid would have been via the arch because the rest of the structure has smooth faces. And there doesn't seem to be any way in through that.'

'Not now, there isn't, I agree,' Aaron Levi said. 'But we know the area around the war memorial suffered great damage. We also know the pyramid wasn't flattened. But what if it suffered structural damage that could have stressed the panel at the back of the arch?'

Falcon knelt down on the flags in front of the arch and passed the torch to Fiona who was standing by his side. 'Can you keep the light on the back panel, please?'

She held the torch steady and Falcon leaned forward and put both of his hands, palms down onto the rear panel. He adjusted his position to give himself the best leverage and pushed hard against the stone. For a long moment nothing happened. Then there was a pneumatic hiss of air being released and the stone fell forward.

For a moment Falcon was caught off balance, but he managed to recover and catch the thin stone slab. He lowered it gently to the ground and leaned it up against the pyramid to the side of the arch.

Then he took the torch back and shone it into the dark space revealed. The tunnel extended backwards for the length of a single sandstone block, and as he peered inside, Falcon could see something lying on the earthen floor of the tunnel. A shadow wrapped in sacking.

Falcon stooped down and started to move into the tunnel towards the shape, but one of the Americans called out an urgent warning.

'Stop. You're moving into great danger. The treasure is always protected.'

For the moment Falcon had forgotten they were there, and he froze at the shout.

'Give me the torch.' One of the men moved forward and Falcon passed the torch to him. 'There.' He shone the beam beyond the shadow and picked out two jars, each about six inches high, positioned one on either side of the sacking. They were black; the one to the right bearing the symbol A and the one to the left Ω in gold letters.

'Alpha and Omega,' he spoke the words in a whisper. 'The Beginning and the End.'

'What's in the jars?' Falcon broke the silence.

'Many years ago, when the treasure was in danger, the Guardians protected it with a substance similar to Greek Fire. If the contents of the two jars come together there will be an explosion followed by a fire.'

'But surely that would destroy the artefact?' Fiona said.

'Yes, but it would have prevented it falling into the wrong hands. Now, everyone outside and I will disconnect the trap.'

'No, way.' Falcon snapped out the words. 'I've no intention of letting that pile of sacks out of my sight.'

The American shrugged. 'As you wish, Chief Inspector. Perhaps you would hold the torch for me.'

Five minutes later as the two men backed out of the tunnel, the American was carrying the pile of sacks in his arms, treasuring it like he would a child. For a moment he almost lost his footing as his shoe caught the entrance stone. It fell onto the ground and cracked into two pieces, but the artefact was safe.

'So let's get this back to police HQ,' Falcon said, as soon as he was in the open again.

'Sorry, but no.' The American carrying the sacking suddenly stopped and gestured with his head.

And six men in black ski suits carrying Uzi sub-machine guns materialized out of the gloom.

For a moment everyone was frozen in a tableau. Then slowly, the men with the guns started to back away, shielding the one carrying the artefact.

'Now, wait a minute.' Falcon stepped forward. One of the men moved in front of him but Falcon knocked his Uzi aside, gambling that the unit didn't want to be responsible for sparking off an international incident in the middle of Garton.

'Put your weapons down. The area's crawling with police. And in any case, I don't think it's in your own interest to generate the negative publicity starting a shooting war would bring.'

Without waiting to reply, one of the Guardians made a gesture with his hand and the others followed him as he disappeared into the gathering murk.

Falcon was on his radio at once.

39

'So there are armed men are on the loose in Garton,' Mallory snapped out the question.

'Yes,' Falcon replied. 'I've put an armed response unit on stand-by, and I've flooded the area around the synagogue with officers. We'll pull them in.'

'Without a bloodbath?' Mallory pressed the point.

'In all honesty, guv, I don't believe they'll use their weapons in public. They shouldn't be armed, sure, but they didn't strike me as being lunatics. Or martyrs either, come to that. No, I just think they were genuinely shocked when they found the artefact was hidden in the pyramid. And they could still—'

He was interrupted as a constable from the front office came onto the platform. 'There's an Aaron Levi here asking to speak to you, sir.'

'Right,' Mallory responded her. 'Bring him down.'

The constable came back a few minutes later bringing Aaron Levi with her. After the incident at the pyramid Mallory had sent him to the synagogue to talk to the Americans.

'Assistant Chief Constable, I'm deeply sorry for what happened out there. I told them they aren't in America now, and that the police over here take a very dim view of guns on the streets. They've asked me to negotiate with you on their behalf.'

'Negotiate?' Mallory repeated the word, the venom clear in his voice. 'We don't negotiate with armed criminals.'

'All they ask is a meeting with the police in the synagogue.'

'And what exactly is the purpose of this meeting?'

Aaron Levi paused, choosing his words carefully. 'You have to understand what finding the artefact after all this time means to the Guardians, and when it was located their first priority was to take it to what they regarded as a more suitable place: the synagogue. If necessary, I believe that they are prepared to fight to protect it. But they really don't want that. So they ask for a deal. They'll hand over their weapons if you'll let them stay in the synagogue and contact the sect headquarters in the States to discuss the way forward.'

Mallory thought for a moment. 'By rights, I should have the bloody lot of them arrested. And I will if they play any more games. But handing over their guns could diffuse the situation and prevent what could well be an international incident, I suppose. But I insist on one thing: the police must be party to all the discussions between the members over here and the sect in America, because anything else they do in Garton must have the full approval of the police.'

'Agreed.' Aaron Levi sounded relieved.

Mallory nodded. 'Thank you. I'll send Dan Logan with armed back-up to supervise the handover of weapons. Once we get the all clear from Dan, we'll go back to the synagogue and start talking to the Guardians themselves.'

Falcon arranged for coffee and sandwiches to be sent up from the canteen. When the food arrived, the team sat at the table eating.

Mallory looked around. 'So for the moment let's forget all this nonsense about the sect and religious artefacts. Where are we now with respect to the real investigation? Gary?'

'I agree, guv, that the religious murders had nothing whatever to do with the Guardians, or any lost artefact. But we can't ignore them now because Debbie Connelly has drawn them into the matrix. She did that because she thought they could get her back on centre stage. So she offered the Guardians a deal. She would reveal the location of their artefact if they would agree to display it at the opening ceremony of the Faith Conference in some way that involved her. As it happens, Debbie Connelly didn't follow-up on the deal. We don't know why she pulled out, but maybe she's gone directly to the TV people. Even so, she doesn't have it herself, so she probably decided to collect it when she felt it was safe to do so.

Probably at night when the area around the war memorial will be clear. So we've set a trap by posting officers around the pyramid.'

'You really think she'll show up there?' Mallory didn't seem convinced.

'It all depends on how important the artefact is to her, and we don't really know that.'

'Fiona?'

'I agree,' she replied. 'We don't know what plans she actually has for the artefact. In fact, there is a whole raft of things we don't know about Debbie, and about Mark DeMasters, come to that. Particularly, the dynamics of their relationship.'

'For instance?' Mallory asked.

'Mark DeMasters and Debbie Connelly are two people feeding off each other. A modern day *Bonnie and Clyde*, if you like. And although we don't know the way their relationship works, we are beginning to get some intriguing indications.'

'What kind of indications?' Falcon asked.

'Debbie Connelly seems to be continually changing, like a chameleon taking on the colour of the background. First, she comes to us and links the mystery play to the murders. A concerned citizen helping the police with their inquiries. And in fact her evidence did lead us to discover the hidden chapel and the body of Sebastian Banks. But that was the end of her involvement with us.'

'Which means she'd stepped off centre stage.' Mallory was beginning to understand where this was going.

'Right, but the point is that she still needs to be centre stage. We've no way of knowing what she had planned originally to get back into the limelight, but everything must have changed when she saw the TV programme. We can only guess here, but I believe Mark DeMasters saw the programme with her and told her what he'd uncovered in the research for his thesis, namely, that he could locate the missing artefact. So she approached the sect, who, incidentally, were featured in the programme, to offer them a deal. But later, she appeared to renege on it. And we don't know why.'

They were still mulling that over when Arthur Fielding came into the operations room. The expression on his face was like the cat that had found the cream.

161

'A breakthrough, Assistant Chief Constable. We found several fingerprints on the spear that had been driven into Sebastian Banks's side. None of them were on record, but as soon as you put Mark DeMasters in the frame for the murder of Sebastian Banks my lads went back to his room, which was still a crime scene, and lifted a series of prints from the handle of his toothbrush, which is a personal object unlikely to be used by anyone else. And bingo. A match. Mark DeMasters's fingerprints were on the spear, mixed in with bloodstains. He had held the spear when there was wet blood on it. And more, the blood was that of Sebastan Banks.'

'Got the bastard.' Mallory slapped Arthur Fielding on the shoulder. 'At last. Evidence to confirm he murdered Sebastian Banks. Fiona was right, we know for certain now which of the two people in the matrix is capable of murder. DeMasters.'

'Yeah, I thought you'd be pleased. And now we're checking Mark DeMasters' prints against all the other crime scenes. I'll let you know the results when I have them, but as of now you can arrest DeMasters in connection with the murder of Sebastian Banks.'

For a moment the elation he felt stayed with Mallory. But he couldn't help wondering why Mark DeMasters had been careless enough to leave his prints in the chapel?

Perhaps being identified as the killer of Sebastian Banks didn't matter to him any more.

40

Fiona paused for a moment and looked around. It was the first time she had ever been in a synagogue, and her initial impression was one of rich deep colours.

The Americans were busy setting up a video contact with the States and Aaron Levi was standing with Fiona and Falcon as they waited for the link to be established. After a few minutes, one of the Guardians approached Aaron Levi and spoke in his ear.

'They're ready to open the link,' Aaron Levi told Falcon. 'You agree for them to go ahead?'

'No problem.'

The video equipment had been set up on a small table. Fiona was used to video links for conferencing procedures, but she wasn't familiar with the state of the art system that had been set up. The web camera, which was positioned on top of a computer, looked different to any Fiona had seen before. Obviously the members of the sect were no strangers to modern technology.

One of the Guardians was sitting in front of the screen tapping a series of commands into the computer via the keyboard. Five of his colleagues, together with Fiona, Falcon and Aaron Levi, stood in a circle waiting. The excitement was palpable, so strong it could almost be felt on the air.

Suddenly the screen seemed to burst into life, and the image of a man appeared. He had a white beard and was dressed like the rest of the sect in a long black coat and white shirt. When he spoke it was in a language Fiona didn't understand.

Aaron Levi stepped up to the web cam. He identified himself

and requested that all conversation take place in English, not Yiddish. The man at the other end of the link seemed to take an age considering the request. Then he nodded.

The tension reached its height as one of the Guardians stepped up to the table. For a moment he stood there, as if he was suddenly unable to move, and Fiona found herself caught up in the drama of the moment as he finally leaned forward and placed the long wooden box containing the artefact on the table. The box was narrow, about two feet long and six inches wide. It was ornately carved, with golden handles at each end in the shape of some kind of animal that Fiona didn't recognize.

He checked with the figure on the screen that the box was visible at his end, then he took out a bunch of keys on a thick ring. Carefully, he selected one of the keys and inserted it into a slot below the right handle. There was a loud click as he turned the key. Then he repeated the operation on the left handle. Finally, he reached forward and lifted the lid of the box.

Inside, Fiona caught a glimpse of white cloth which was lifted out and draped across the American's arm. As he did so, there was a sharp intake of breath from Aaron Levi, and the figure on the screen began to intone a prayer.

'What is it?' Fiona whispered the question to Aaron Levi.

'*The Breastplate of Judgement*. Found again after all those centuries.'

And he, too, began to pray.

The Guardians were still praying and talking excitedly over the video link with their leader in America, making sure he could see what the box had contained.

Aaron Levi drew Fiona and Falcon to one side. 'This is a great find. One of the most sacred relics in all the history of Judaism.'

'So what exactly is this *Breastplate of Judgement*?' Falcon asked him.

'When Moses came down from Mount Sinai he carried with him the tablets of the Ten Commandments. Moses was given instructions on how to build the Ark of the Covenant to house the tablets. But it is also written that Moses carried a list of twelve precious stones, one each for the twelve tribes of Israel, and these stones had to be set in *The Breastplate of Judgement*, which had to be worn by the first high priest, Aaron, brother of Moses.'

'And the breastplate itself?' Fiona asked.

'As you can see.' Aaron Levi inclined his head towards the garment held up to the camera by one of the Guardians. 'It's a square made out of embroidered linen with threads of gold, purple and scarlet. The stones themselves are in four rows of three. It was worn across the heart of the high priest, suspended from the shoulders by gold chains. From the lower corners, it was attached by blue ribbons; the stones are secured to the breastplate by golden settings. The origin of the stones themselves is unclear, but it's thought they may have once belonged to Lucifer. In the breastplate they carry the names of the twelve tribes of Israel. Some authorities believe that eventually the breastplate itself became worn out, but from what we have here, it doesn't look like it. Another theory tells that the breastplate was lost with the Ark of the Covenant.'

'But what's the great importance of the breastplate?' Fiona asked.

'It was used in divination; some believe that it could reveal the will of God directly to the high priest and so to his people.'

'How?' Fiona asked.

'We are not entirely clear, but some scholars think that letters in the names of the twelve tribes light up and in this way convey the word of God to the high priest.'

Fiona seemed stunned. 'You believe the breastplate does this?' She asked.

Aaron Levi smiled, a gentle smile that lit up his face. 'I believe it did once fulfil the role of judgement. But for it to work now, many conditions must be fulfilled. But one in particular, perhaps.'

'And what is that?'

'The return of the Ark of the Tabernacle to the Chosen People.'

'You mean, the breastplate won't work on its own?'

Aaron Levi smiled again, this time at Fiona's choice of words. 'I think *won't work* gives the wrong impression of it. It's not an instrument that performs a mechanical or an electrical function. It is more, perhaps, an idea. A concept. But however it functions, it holds a very special sacred place in the hearts of all the Jewish people.'

'And what will happen to it now?' Fiona found herself gazing again at the long hidden artefact that had played such a vital role in the history of the Jews.

Aaron Levi shrugged. 'No doubt, there will be many questions asked. Where should the breastplate be kept for safekeeping until the Ark is also returned? What should its role be in the present century? Many questions.'

At that moment, one of the Americans came over and drew Aaron Levi aside. When he returned he led Fiona and Falcon back to the plasma screen, explaining that the leader of the sect wanted to talk to them over the video link.

The operator made some adjustments to the picture, using commands on the keyboard, then he moved out of the way so the camera could centre on Fiona and Falcon.

'Good evening, as I believe it is over there.' The accent was Eastern European, laced strongly with American. 'My name is Shimon Stein, and I am the leader of the sect which guarded *The Breastplate of Judgement*. Can you please introduce yourselves?'

'I am Detective Chief Inspector Gary Falcon, Garton Police, and this is Dr Fiona Nightingale, who is a clinical psychologist working with us. We are part of a murder investigation team.'

'Thank you. I have been told about the investigation. And that one of your suspects, a young lady as I understand it, has expressed an interest in using the breastplate for her own purpose.'

'Yes, although she had no idea that it was *The Breastplate of Judgement*.'

'So what did she want with it?'

Falcon explained about the Faith Conference and that in the opinion of the police Debbie Connelly intended to attempt to hi-jack the opening ceremony. There was a long pause on the other end of the link as the leader considered what Falcon had told him. Then he sighed.

'Thank you for being up front with us, Detective Chief Inspector. The safety of the breastplate is, of course, our paramount concern. But we cannot ignore the prophecy that has been handed down to the Guardians from generation to generation.'

'What prophecy?' Falcon asked.

'That a sign will be revealed to us when the time is right to reveal *The Breastplate of Judgement* to the world.'

'And is there such a sign now?' Aaron Levi almost whispered the words.

For a moment there was silence. 'Yes, we believe there is. The *Birkat Hachama*.'

'Of course,' Aaron Levi said. 'The festival.'

'What is it?' Fiona asked.

'A ceremony in which Jews recite the *Blessing of the Sun*.' Aaron Levi replied. 'It is based on the fact that every twenty-eight years the sun returns to the same position it held during the time of Creation. And that will happen this year, 2009, on the 8th of April. The day we now know is the opening ceremony of the Faith Conference in your city. It is without doubt, a sign. And the importance of the Breastplate to Jews around the world cannot be overestimated. It will be a great day indeed when it is revealed. One of the biggest religious events ever staged.'

The Greatest Show On Earth, Fiona thought. And Debbie Connelly wants to be at the centre of it.

41

The shadows around the pyramid had lengthened until it was impossible to make out the base. But the watchers, designated units Alpha One and Alpha Two, were in place, at either stretch of the road where the war memorial was sited. In addition, the surrounding area was under tight surveillance as the police waited for Debbie Connelly or Mark DeMasters to come looking for the artefact.

The stretch of road was well lit and fairly busy with container lorries moving in and out of the port, but there was only the occasional pedestrian around at this time of night.

'Alpha Two, to control,' the voice came over the radio.

'Control, go ahead Alpha Two.'

'There's a female, late forties to fifties, approaching from the north. It looks like a bag lady. She's carrying something and she's staggering over the pavement. Wait.' There was a short silence. 'There's someone else with her. He's just come out of the shadows. Looks like a tramp.'

'Got that, Alpha Two. A tramp and a bag lady. We'll track them in.'

The Alpha Two unit stayed in the shadows on the opposite side of the road to the pyramid and watched the man and woman approach. The man seemed reasonably sober, but the woman was weaving across the pavement and, as she came closer, the Alpha Two unit could hear her singing in a raucous voice.

The tramp tried to catch her arm, but she evaded him and continued along the pavement. Then she spotted the war memorial and staggered up to the steps. She started to climb them, then apparently thought better of it and sat down. She took a long drink from a bottle she was carrying in a brown paper bag, then offered it to the tramp.

'In a minute.' The members of the Alpha Two unit caught the words. 'Just take a leak first.'

The bag lady cackled and took another long swig from the bottle.

'Shit, that's all we need.' The sergeant in command of Alpha Two cursed under his breath. 'When the tramp gets back they're going to have a drinking session on the steps.'

'Shall we move them on?' one of his men asked.

'Yes. Threaten to arrest them. Anything. But get the buggers out of the way.'

The officer was halfway across the road when there was an explosion and a flash of flame leapt upwards from somewhere inside the pyramid.

And a figure danced down the steps screaming, his body enveloped in a throbbing blue-edged sheet of flame.

'All right.' Mallory looked around. 'What happened?'

'It's not entirely certain yet, but we can get the broad picture.' Falcon did not sound pleased.

'The area was under surveillance and two teams were watching the road approaches to the war memorial. At around half past nine a male and a female, who were tagged as a bag lady and a tramp, came along the road towards the war memorial. We can assume now that the female was Debbie Connelly, and let's face it, she's an actress. So it would be no sweat for her to assume the role of a bag lady. Anyway, when they got to the war memorial the female sat down on the steps and started drinking from a bottle. She asked the male to join her, but he said he was going around the back of the pyramid to take a leak. He was lost in the shadows then, but he must have seen the broken stone and gone into the pyramid. The next moment there was a burst of fire and the male came running onto the road in a sheet of flame. We found later that the jars had been tipped over and we can only surmise that he'd set off the fire trap. This was later confirmed by the presence of scorch marks on the flags inside the passage. Officers from Alpha One and Two responded, calling for an ambulance and doing what they could for the male.'

'What happened to the woman?' Mallory asked.

'She wasn't injured, but she hung around and said she'd go to hospital in the ambulance with the man.'

'Did she give any details about him?'

Falcon shook his head. 'No, she said she'd only met him that night. But she was concerned enough to go to the hospital with him.'

'I bet she was. What better way to get away from the scene than in an official vehicle. So what happened at the hospital?'

'The male was taken into A&E, and naturally everything there was concentrated on him. While all that was happening the woman she said she wanted to go to the toilet, and then legged it out of a window.'

'Didn't anyone think that she might have needed an escort?' Mallory cursed.

'Oh, yes, they did. And a female officer escorted her to the toilet. But the woman clobbered her with the bottle she was apparently still carrying.'

'So the woman got away from the war memorial by going in the ambulance, and then left the hospital via the toilet.' Mallory sighed and shook his head. 'And the male? Presumably it's Mark DeMasters?'

'We don't know yet, but it's odds on that it is him.'

'So how is he?'

'Not badly burned, due in no small measure to the actions of the officers on the scene who managed to smother much of the flames.'

'So, we can assume that DeMasters went into the pyramid and inadvertently set off the fire trap. But why was the trap left in place?' Mallory asked.

'Forensics wanted to go over the scene. But they couldn't work it as a crime scene in case it warned off Debbie Connelly and Mark DeMasters. So it was agreed that everything should be left in place while the pyramid was being used to draw in the suspects. And under normal circumstances we would have moved in before they could have set off the trap.'

'So we had Debbie Connelly under our hand,' Mallory said. 'Again.'

'Looks that way, guv.' Falcon agreed.

'OK, so she's still out there on the streets. But let's be positive about this, we've got our prime suspect in custody at the hospital. So the trap was a success.'

'To that extent, yes. It was a success.' Unlike Mallory, Fiona didn't sound up-beat.

'But?' Mallory waited.

'But now we know that Debbie Connelly really is a chameleon, because she's using her theatre skills to stay hidden. She can disappear into the general population at will. And that could make her a very dangerous animal.'

'OK, but two of the original three people involved on this case are out of the matrix now. Sebastian Banks is dead, and Mark DeMasters is in custody. So will Debbie Connelly carry on with whatever it was she had planned?'

'The crucial question,' Fiona replied. 'I don't know the answer, but I suggest we interview DeMasters as soon as possible. He holds the key now.'

42

The white-coated doctor stood outside the intensive care unit facing Falcon and Fiona. A third figure waited in the background.

'I've only agreed to let you talk to the patient because you told me that he may have information vital to your murder investigation, so I'll give you ten minutes. But I have to say that he's heavily sedated, and you might get nothing at all out of him.'

Inside the unit there was a world of flashing signals and soft dim lights, the quiet broken only by bleeping monitors.

The doctor led them to a cubicle by the door. Inside, a plastic tent had been rigged over a bed and a nurse wearing a mask was sitting with a patient who was propped into a sitting position, his back protected by a cage. Much of his torso was wrapped in silver coated sheeting, but his face seemed to have escaped the fire. He was hooked up to several monitors, and a tube ran into a port in his wrist, constantly drip-feeding sedatives.

'Is he awake?' the doctor asked.

The nurse stood up. 'Just about, but he keeps moving in and out of consciousness.'

The doctor turned to Falcon. 'We don't know yet what caused the accident, but on the basis of what your people told us we're assuming it was a chemical agent. The burns are second degree and are not as extensive as we first thought, and although there's been an amount of smoke inhalation there's minimum airways damage.'

'So his condition's not life threatening?' Falcon said.

'No, but as a precaution we've put him in a tent to minimize early stage infection and treat him for shock. We're not a major burns unit, but we're taking advice from the unit at the White Cross Hospital in Manchester and as soon as we can arrange suitable transport we'll transfer him there.'

'So how can we talk to him if he's in the tent?' Falcon asked.

'No problem. This type of tent is rigged for communication and you can speak to the patient through a built-in microphone system. I've already set it up. But before we begin there are two questions I'd like to put to you.'

'Go ahead.'

'We couldn't find any identification on the patient, but you say you think his name is Mark DeMasters; can you confirm that please?'

Falcon stepped forward and looked at the man's face through the plastic sheeting, mentally comparing it with the photograph that had been supplied by the university.

'Yes, it's Mark DeMasters. And the other question?'

'When I agreed to let you talk to Mr DeMasters I stipulated two people only. To save the patient undue stress. Now I see there are three of you.' He left it hanging as a question.

'Yes, sorry about that, Doctor. But this is a difficult situation. As I said, we have good reason to believe that your patient can provide information vital to our investigation. But anything he does provide must be fireproof - no pun intended. So we must be very careful to follow protocols. We don't want any smart lawyer raising questions about the legality of the evidence, do we?'

'I suppose not, no.'

'So I've arranged for Mr Dayton to be present. He's tonight's duty solicitor at police HQ, and he's agreed to represent Mark DeMasters. It offers safeguards all round.'

The doctor didn't seem entirely convinced, but he didn't argue.

'Mr DeMasters,' the doctor said into the microphone on the trolley. 'The police are here. Do you agree to talk to them?'

There was a long silence, then a croak that seemed to float into the air. The nurse picked up a cup from the bedside table and placed the straw sticking out of it between the patient's lips. For a few moments he drank greedily, then nodded his head and the nurse took the cup away.

'Do you agree to talk to the police?' The doctor repeated the question.

'Oh, yes, I'll talk to them.' The voice was faint and rasping.

'Thank you.' Falcon hid his surprise at DeMasters' willingness to talk to them and took a tape recorder from his shoulder bag. He placed the recorder on the bedside table outside the plastic tent.

'Is this really necessary?' Dr Mandon asked.

'Absolutely.' Falcon placed two tapes into the machine. 'May I call you Mark?'

'I suppose so.'

'Good. Now we'd like to ask you a few questions. But first I have to point out to you that you will be interviewed under caution, and as such you are entitled to have a legal representative present. I have provided you with a suitable representative and he is here now. His name is Peter Dayton. He is here to look after your interests, and because of the present circumstances, he has agreed to the interview going ahead without speaking to you himself in private first. But he can stop the interview at any time he likes if he feels it is compromising your rights. Do you agree to this?'

'Yes.' Just the one word.

'Thank you.' Falcon formally cautioned Mark DeMasters, then turned on the tape recorder and went through the formalities. Then he leaned forward and spoke into the microphone on the trolley.

'Mark, when did you first meet Debbie Connelly?'

'When Sebastian Banks was helping me to come to terms with my problems over religion. Debbie was directing a piece of street theatre for Seb.'

'And what is your relationship with Debbie? Is she your girlfriend?'

Silence, and Falcon began to think that Mark DeMasters wasn't going to answer. Then the croaking voice again.

'At first I thought she was my girlfriend. She's very pretty, you know.'

Fiona leaned forward. Falcon sensed her interest and let her lead.

'Yes, Debbie is pretty, Mark. Very pretty. So you fell for her, right?'

'Yes.'

'Have you had many girlfriends?'

'No.' He almost snarled out the word, catching Fiona by surprise.

'Why didn't you bother with girls, Mark?'

'I believed sex was wrong. Dirty.'

Fiona nodded to herself. It must have been part of his father's fanatical creed. A part that had twisted the boy's mind. Filled him with feelings of guilt. So much so that the effect of someone as glamorous as Debbie Connelly on an inexperienced boy like Mark DeMasters must have been devastating.

But something still wasn't right. Something about the relationship between the two of them didn't quite gel.

'Mark.' Falcon took over the questioning. 'For the past few days you and Debbie have been on the run, right?'

'Yes.'

'Can you tell us where you've been hiding out?' Falcon half expected Dayton to block that question, but he didn't.

'We've been staying in one of the portacabins behind the Anglican cathedral. There are three cabins there to store material to be used in the Faith Festival.'

'And how did you have access to the cabin?'

'Stuff for the mystery play is stored there and Debbie has a key.' The last few words were dragged out. He started to cough again.

'Did Debbie change as you got to know each other?' Fiona asked, still worried that she was missing something in the relationship between the two of them. 'Did she start telling you what to do?'

'Yes. She started treating me differently. Like she despised me. As if I was rubbish.' The answers came out in a staccato succession, as if his mind was running ahead unchecked.

Typical control behaviour, Fiona thought. Dominate someone, then despise them for allowing it to happen.

But the key question still remained; why did Debbie Connelly want to dominate him?

43

'Mark.' Fiona kept her voice soft. 'You know about the murders of the religious leaders?'

'Yes.' Nothing else.

Peter Dayton leaned forward, alerted by the question. But for the moment he remained silent.

'What do you think about the murders? About someone killing religious leaders?'

'They deserved it.' This time the response was more positive.

'What do you mean, they deserved it?' Falcon came in quickly before Dayton could shut him down.

'They were liars. All liars. They led people astray with their false beliefs. They tormented people, took away their happiness. They did that to my sister. They killed her. All off them. They're evil.' Mark DeMasters was shouting now, and the nurse had to hold him down as his voice resonated across the ward.

It was almost as if he was two personalities, Fiona thought. The meek, docile student of the everyday world and the aggressive, violent killer released by the death of his sister.

'Is that what Seb thought?' Fiona asked.

DeMasters sighed, his control coming back. 'No, Seb was helping me. He was showing me the way to open my heart to true faith.'

'So what went wrong?' Fiona asked.

There was a long silence this time. Drawn out until Fiona thought Mark DeMasters had drifted away from them.

Then, eventually, he spoke again. 'My sister died. That's what happened. And it was my father's fault.'

'So what did you do after your sister's death?' Falcon asked.

'Sorry, but I can't allow that question,' Peter Dayton interceded.

'All right. But did you tell Debbie about your sister?' Falcon approached the question another way.

'Yes.'

'And what did she say?'

'She told me I should take revenge for Isabel's death. That if I didn't I would be a failure. A weakling people would always laugh at.'

'And what happened then?' Dayton let the question stand, hoping the answer would favour his client.

'We hatched a plot.'

'The two of you did?'

'Yes, the two of us. But Debbie was the one with the ideas.'

'And what did this plot involve?'

'Stop.'

Peter Dayton tried to halt that line of questioning, but Mark DeMasters ignored him.

'We intended to kill the three religious leaders.'

'Mark, I strongly caution you to stop now.'

But the damage had been done, and the full significance of the bombshell hit Fiona. So far, like the rest of the team, she'd assumed that Mark DeMasters had been the driving force behind the God Slayer murders. An act of revenge triggered by the tragic death of his sister. Now it was becoming clear that it had been an act of revenge, yes, but not an act dreamed up by Mark DeMasters. In the fragile state of mind brought on by the death of his sister he may have carried out the actual killings, Fiona acknowledged, but all the time Debbie Connelly had been in the background pulling the strings. Praying on a vulnerable personality.

Peter Dayton was watching closely now, poised to object again if he thought DeMasters was incriminating himself.

'What about Sebastian Banks?' Falcon asked. 'Why was he killed?'

'I advise you not to answer that question,' Peter Dayton came in. But again Mark DeMasters ignored him, and Fiona almost felt sympathy for the lawyer.

'Seb found out about the murders. Debbie tried to keep him on side, but he threatened to go to the police.'

'So you killed him?'

Dayton came in at once, and this time DeMasters took his advice and refused to answer the question.

'OK, Mark.' Fiona came in on another tack. 'Debbie continued to drip-feed information to the police, keeping herself in the limelight. And she took us as far as locating the hidden chapel. But she was no use to us after that, so what did she plan to do then?'

'Everything we did was centred around the mystery play. The monks fighting the unbelievers, the hidden chapel, the Crucifixion, all of it. Then at the end St George slays the dragon. But Debbie switched it so the dragon won the fight. I was to be in the dragon costume and after the victory I was going to take the dragon onto the cathedral steps where Debbie was to join me. For a few moments she would stand in front of all the people waving a large flag with a dragon image on it to show the supremacy of the Devil.'

'And what was to happen next?' Fiona asked.

'The climax. One last role for the dragon. Debbie would already have doused herself in petrol and, as she threw the banner into the crowd I was to light a blowtorch hidden in the dragon costume and send a jet of flame through the creature's mouth and set Debbie ablaze on the cathedral steps.'

In that instant, Fiona realized the full scope of Debbie Connelly's plan. Right from the start she'd used everyone around her with one aim always in mind: to stage a spectacular finale.

'And what about you?' Fiona asked.

'Debbie told me I could get away in the panic and confusion. But I planned to stay with her. I would never have abandoned her.'

So that was why he wasn't bothered if his prints were found in the chapel, Falcon thought. Mark DeMasters never intended to get away. He'd chosen to remain at the side of his girlfriend.

44

'Are we to understand that Debbie Connelly plans to commit suicide.' Falcon sounded as if he didn't quite believe it.

'Ritual suicide, yes. It seems that's what she intended,' Fiona replied.

'But why?'

'We don't know that yet. Mark, do you know if anything happened to Debbie? Anything that might have driven her to suicide?'

'No. She never talked about things like that.'

'But you were partners, weren't you?'

'I thought so, at first. We planned things together.'

'What kind of things?' Falcon came in like a shot, sensing a confession. But there was no answer from DeMasters.

'Mark, you said you and Debbie were partners *at first*. What did you mean by that?' Fiona took up the questioning.

'She changed everything. Cut me out of the action.'

'When did she cut you out?'

'After we'd watched the TV programme on a Jewish sect searching for a lost artefact in the James Street synagogue.'

'Why should that be of any interest to Debbie?'

'In the TV programme they said the artefact was of very special importance because it allowed people to talk directly to God. But it was lost, and the reporter told the story of what happened the night the artefact went missing. About how the two men guarding it were found dead in a house hit by a bomb, but the artefact itself had disappeared. And the reporter explained that a team of sect members had come to Garton to search for it.'

'But I still don't understand why this should interest Debbie,' Fiona said.

'Because I told her I knew where it was hidden.'

'And how did you know that?'

'My undergraduate thesis was on religious symbols in Garton architecture, and at one stage I found a reference to some special symbolism in an old church by the docks. The church had been demolished in the 1930s, but I thought there might have been something in the parish records.'

He paused, indicating that he wanted another drink and the nurse held the straw for him.

'I was allowed to search through the records and I found a wartime diary written by a curate at the church. It was a fascinating document, and I read all of it. In one entry, the curate described what happened during one bombing raid. He'd just left the church when he'd seen two men approach the nearby pyramid war memorial and carry an object up the steps. The curate thought it was probably something to do with the black market, and he left then to comfort his parishioners in a nearby bomb shelter. Apparently, he wrote the incident in his diary, but when he went to check the pyramid the following day there was no sign that it had been tampered with, and the curate thought they must have moved the object somewhere else.'

It was all beginning to fall into place now, Fiona thought.

'So what did Debbie do when you told her you knew where the artefact was?' Fiona asked.

'She was over the moon. She said that unveiling it would make the perfect finale to her show.' There was a change in the tone of his voice that Falcon seized on.

'Weren't you pleased with that?'

'No.' The single word was snarled out.

'Why?'

'Because that's what it had become suddenly: *her* show.' There was bitterness in his voice as he emphasized the word. 'Until then we'd planned things together, and I was prepared to stay with her on the cathedral steps. I would have done that for her. But everything changed when the Americans and the artefact came on the scene.'

'How do mean, changed?' Falcon asked.

'She intended to offer them a deal. She would bring them the artefact if they agreed to display it in her presence at the opening ceremony of the Faith Conference.'

'And what about you?' Falcon wanted to be clear.

'Oh, yes, what about me? I'll tell you what about me, shall I? Nothing. She intended to dump me. After all the things I'd done for her.'

So that was why Mark DeMasters had been prepared to open up to them, Falcon thought, because he'd been betrayed. But there was still one question that needed an answer.

'Mark, if you knew that Debbie was going to cut you out of the loop, why did you agree to go to the pyramid with her to locate the artefact?'

'Hah.'

The word exploded from his lips and set off a hacking cough. When he'd brought his breathing under control again, he laughed. A cackling laugh that was almost indistinguishable from the cough caused by smoke inhalation.

'Why did I go to the pyramid with her? I'll tell you why, because I was going to destroy it.'

The coughing started again, but this time the nurse placed an oxygen mask over his mouth and nose.

And at that stage the doctor ended the interview.

45

'So how did it go?' Mallory asked the question when Falcon and Fiona were back in the major incident room.

'Very well, considering DeMasters' condition. It's not life threatening, but he's still very weak,' Falcon replied. 'He drifted away in the end, but not before he sang like a canary.'

'Why would he do that?'

'Because all is apparently not well in the camp. According to DeMasters, Debbie was about to dump him.'

Falcon repeated what Mark DeMasters had told them about Debbie Connelly's plans to stage a show at the opening ceremony of the Faith Conference.

'And she intended cutting him out of it? You sure of that?' Mallory asked.

'Absolutely. There was no role for our boy once the Guardians came on the scene.'

'And he didn't take kindly to that?'

'He certainly did not. To the extent that he was prepared to destroy the artefact.'

'All this fits in with the other stuff he told us,' Fiona said. 'Particularly when he dropped the bombshell.'

'You mean, he admitted to the murders?'

'He admitted that he *intended* to carry out the murders. And he might have actually gone all the way and admitted to them, but his brief pulled him up short.'

'Then what was this bombshell?'

'We'd assumed that Mark DeMasters set-up the murders of the

three religious leaders as an act of revenge on all religion following the death of his sister. A death which he blamed on his father. But it turns out that although Mark probably wielded the lances that were responsible for the actual killings, the strings were being pulled by Debbie Connelly. She taunted DeMasters into carrying out the murders.'

'But why?' Mallory asked.

'We can't be sure of the reason yet, but according to her doctor at the Hayfield Clinic something had affected her behaviour and set her back on the slippery slope. He started to get close to finding out what it was, but she didn't confide in him and in the end she discharged herself from the clinic. Then some time later, she met Mark DeMasters and hatched the plot to kill the religious leaders. A gigantic production. Designed to put her centre stage.'

'You called it a production,' Mallory said.

'And that's what it was, theatre on a grand scale, and it was all run to a careful design. First, she identified the monks' robes for us. Then she led us to the hidden chapel and the body of Sebastian Banks. After that, according to DeMasters, Debbie intended to stage the final act by setting fire to herself on the cathedral steps, leaving DeMasters to get away in the confusion.'

'So that was why she was so interested in helping with the mystery play. To turn it to her own ends,' Mallory said.

'Yes, but then she changed plans and switched her attention to the Guardians. Because if she could get hold of the artefact she could achieve the notoriety she obviously craved by appearing some way in the opening ceremony. No, Debbie Connelly – little Miss butter-wouldn't-melt-in-her-mouth – was as much responsible for the murders as if she'd wielded the lances herself.'

'Christ, and she's the one still out on the streets. Anything else?'

'DeMasters told us they'd been hiding out in a portacabin in the grounds of the Anglican cathedral. And before you ask, I've already sent Dan Logan down there with a unit to stake the place out.'

'So she might just fall into the trap?'

'She might, but I wouldn't hold your breath. Debbie Connelly knows we've got DeMasters in custody. So, if she's smart, and I think she's very smart, she'll assume he's talked to the police and she'll give the portacabin a wide berth.'

'So we messed up and let Debbie Connelly slip through our fingers yet again, and as a result she's out there on the street now planning God knows what. We have to go back and re-interview DeMasters. See if he can give us anything else on Debbie Connelly's plans. And we have to do it as soon as the doctor allows it.'

But unfortunately the doctor couldn't allow it. Because Mark DeMasters died later that night.

46

'How did it happen?' Mallory asked at the morning briefing. 'You said that the burns Mark DeMasters suffered weren't life threatening.'

'They weren't.' Goldilocks had taken the call from the hospital. 'Mark DeMasters died of a completely unrelated heart problem. Apparently, it was an accident just waiting to happen. Had been for years.'

'Just our bloody luck that it happened last night.'

One of the detectives working the investigation came over to the table. 'Guv, there's a call come in from a DCI on the West Country force. He wants to speak to the SIO running the God Slayer investigation. Says he might have some important information.'

'Thanks.' Falcon turned to Goldilocks. 'Can you patch the call though here and put it on the speakers, please?'

Goldilocks moved in front of an impressive-looking phone console and pressed a series of buttons. Then she handed Falcon the receiver.

'Hello, this is DCI Gary Falcon, SIO for the investigation.'

'Hi.' The voice boomed out over the speaker system and Goldilocks adjusted the volume.

'Sorry, a bit loud at this end.'

'No problem. I'm DCI Bill Thurston, West Country. And I think I may have some info for you.'

'Go ahead, Bill. We could definitely use a breakthrough.'

'Like that, is it?' He obviously detected something in Falcon's tone. 'I know the feeling well. Anyway, let me explain how we come into it. A couple of months ago we were investigating an assault charge. The victim was an actress in a play that was running down here in Plymouth. Apparently, there was some kind of squabble among the cast and the leading lady was sacked. At that stage she assaulted the actress who took over from her. The injured actress reported the assault and we opened an investigation. As I said, the prime suspect was the leading lady and we tried to locate her at the address provided by the theatre company, but apparently, she hadn't shown up there since the assault. At that stage I have to say the case wasn't exactly top of our priority list. You know how it is.'

'For sure, I know,' Falcon agreed. 'Most effective resource management and all that crap.'

'Exactly. But it turned out that the uncle of the actress who was assaulted is a High Court judge, and the pressure came down on us from on high. The upshot was that we moved the investigation up the priority list, and found another address for the actress who was sacked. We decided to bring her in for questioning, and this is where you people come in. The actress who lost her job was Debbie Connelly, and the new address we had for her was in a village on the edge of Garton, but when we contacted the local force to confirm this, all hell broke loose. Apparently, Debbie Connelly is a prime suspect in the God Slayer murders.'

'You know about the murders then?'

'We may be at the end of the known world here, but we have got TV you know.'

Falcon grinned. 'Black and white, I suppose?'

'Cheeky bugger.'

Mallory was getting impatient, but he was well aware that Falcon was building a relationship with his fellow DCI. It could make everything a lot easier that way.

'So, OK, you're right, Bill. Debbie Connelly's in the frame. We think that together with a student named Mark DeMasters, she was responsible for the murders. Can you give us any more details on the assault charge?'

'The play was on a try-out, before opening a run in the West End. Anyway, Miss Connelly was the leading lady, but a review in the local paper absolutely crucified her, to the extent that it finished off by stressing that the only way the play would ever reach the West End, was if the leading lady was changed. Apparently, this was only the tip of the iceberg, because for some time it had been obvious that she wasn't really up to the job. So the producers appointed another leading lady from the cast, and sacked her. Two days later the alleged assault took place.'

'Do you have a copy of the review of the play that appeared in the local paper?' Fiona asked.

'Yes, I can fax it up to you. Is it important?'

'Oh, yes, it's important. It might just provide the key that gets us into Debbie Connelly's mind.'

'Here.' Goldilocks handed Fiona the fax message as it came off the screen.

Fiona read the sheet, then shook her head. 'Oh boy. Talk about putting the knife in.' She handed the sheet to Mallory. 'It's been copied straight from the local newspaper.'

The Wheel.

There is no doubt that this play, set in a small village in rural Norfolk, is a powerful evocation of the changing life of the countryside in the years following the First World War. Centred around the watermill, the play tells the story of the Lasby family and their struggle for survival at a time when the countryside is changing beyond recognition. Matthew Lasby, the head of the family, had been badly wounded in the war and is only present as a shadowy figure lying in his bed. It is the women of the family who bear the brunt of change, and the water wheel is a symbol for their struggle as the mill they run becomes outdated in the face of modern farming practices.

The play requires a powerful figure to hold the family together, a lynchpin for the drama that builds up around them. Unfortunately, the lead player, Debbie Connelly, fails woefully to provide that lynchpin. In all my years reviewing plays, I have never witnessed a performance of such ineptitude. There can be no excuse for this, and clearly Miss Connelly is not suited for a career treading the boards.

The play has great potential but the only way this reviewer can see it ever reaching the West End is to change the leading lady.

James Barbisque, Theatre Critic.

'You were right. Wow. This guy doesn't mince his words.' Mallory passed the sheet to Falcon. 'Fiona what kind of affect would this have had on Connelly?'

'Devastating. Absolutely devastating. This was obviously Debbie's great breakthrough, starring as leading lady in a play that was destined for the West End. Everything she'd ever hoped for. It must have seemed like her birthday and Christmas all rolled into one. The chance to show the world that she was someone. At last. Then the review. It must have destroyed her self-esteem completely. In a very public way.'

'So what did she do?' Mallory asked.

'Well, first off, she apparently assaulted the actress who replaced her. Then after that, it's my guess that she at least tried to fight her demons and made one last attempt to come to terms with her life. That was when she went into the Hayfield Clinic. Dr Martin told us he thought that some event had brought things to a head, but when they finally got close to it in the therapy sessions she backed off and discharged herself.'

'Are you saying she was prepared to commit suicide just because of a bad review of the play she was in?' Mallory sounded sceptical.

'It wasn't just a bad review: it was a very public humiliation that tore away the last vestiges of hope on which she'd built her future. A career in acting. After that there was nothing left for her, except to act out one final role centre stage. That's what everything has been about. That was why she teamed up with Mark DeMasters in the first place. He was another troubled soul, but one she could dominate. She was the ringmaster, and he was the performer.'

'She would go to the extent of planning to kill just because she was disappointed about the way her life was developing?' This time it was Falcon who sounded puzzled.

'No.' Fiona shook her head emphatically. 'No, not just because she was *disappointed*. Disappointed doesn't come anywhere close to describing the emotions Debbie felt after that review. She was always a brittle personality, with a deep-seated desire for recognition. She couldn't face being a failure, and challenged that by becoming an actress, a career that would keep putting her centre stage. So she put all her hopes into it. Only to have them destroyed. As far as she's concerned, she's no more than an empty shell now. But it's a very dangerous empty shell because once acting was out of the picture she needed something else to fill it. And she found it in Mark DeMasters.'

'But why the religious leaders?' Falcon seemed determined to push the question.

'Oh, from what we've learned recently I don't think Debbie was at all bothered that the victims were religious. She simply used Mark DeMasters' hatred of the church to set up the grand scheme which would put her in the limelight. That's what I meant when I said she was a very dangerous empty shell.'

47

'So what now?' Falcon asked Fiona.

'First thing to remember is whatever Debbie does from here on in, she knows she's very much on her own. Even if she doesn't find out Mark DeMasters is dead, she knows he's in custody. Second thing to remember is that she can hide in a crowd by disguising herself.'

'What about this "public show" she was planning with DeMasters? Will she still go on with that?'

'Oh, yes. She'll put herself in the limelight. She's too far gone to alter it.'

At that moment, a red light flashed on the phone console. Goldilocks lifted the receiver and listened for a moment.

'Wait, please.' She turned to Mallory. 'The reporter from the TV company that ran the artefact story is on the line. Apparently, Debbie Connelly has contacted the station and wants to be interviewed.'

'So, she's coming out of the shadows.' Fiona muttered.

'Put the reporter on the speaker.' Mallory sounded upbeat for the first time that evening.

'Hello?' It was a young woman with a strong northern accent. Mallory thought he recognized the voice from TV.

'You're through to the major incident room at Garton police HQ, and this is Assistant Chief Constable Mallory speaking. Can you identify yourself, please?'

'Yes, I'm Mary Franklin, a reporter on Northern Vista television.'

'Thank you. I understand that you have been contacted by

Debbie Connelly?'

'Yes, she's offered us an exclusive.'

'Are you aware that we want to interview her in connection with our investigation?'

'Yes, I am aware of that, it's been in the media. But she came to us, remember. So there's no way we could be accused of harbouring a suspect. Our legal people have checked.'

I bet they have, Mallory thought, but before he could continue that line of questioning Falcon made a cutting gesture with his hand to get his attention. 'Ask if Debbie Connelly is still in contact.'

'No, she's not.' The reporter had picked up Falcon's question over the speaker net.

'OK.' Mallory came on again. 'Can you please tell us how the contact was made?'

'By phone, mobile, I think.'

'This could be a hoax, couldn't it?'

'Yes, it could. We get a lot of hoax calls, particularly when there's a major murder investigation underway. But look at it like this: if it's a hoax, it's a hoax, but if it's real, it could be one hell of a story.'

'So why contact us? Why not keep it exclusive? In my experience, reporters don't exactly line up to share their stories.'

'Tut, tut, Assistant Chief Constable. A tad cynical. But true. However, I don't have any choice this time, because Debbie Connelly wants someone else to take part in the interview.'

'Who's that?' Mallory asked.

'The psychiatrist working for the police: Fiona Nightingale.'

'What?' The word escaped before Fiona could stop it.

'Fiona Nightingale?'

'Yes.'

'OK, Debbie insists that you be there. Apparently, she's already talked to you.'

'But why does she want to speak to me again?'

'She refused to say.'

'How does she want the interview to take place?' Falcon asked.

'Over the phone. Debbie says we'll know how to rig-up a three-way call system.'

'And how does she intend to contact you?'

'She'll ring back to the TV centre switchboard at the half past ten this evening.'

Falcon looked over at Fiona. 'You want to do this?'

'Yes, I don't see why not.' The shock had worn off now. 'But I can't see what she has to gain by opening a dialogue with me.'

'OK, so we'll set this up.' Falcon thought for a moment, then spoke to Mary Franklin. 'But it might help if you come to police HQ. We can route everything through here from your switchboard and this way you and Fiona will be in eye contact, with the rest of the investigation team present here if needed.'

'What you mean is that this way you will have total control of the situation.'

Falcon didn't bother to argue. 'We have specialized equipment already in place here.'

'All right, but I insist on a copy of the interview tape. A full copy to do what I want with.'

'Agreed,' Mallory answered, 'provided none of your actions puts the investigation in jeopardy.'

'I'll go along with that.'

It was a working compromise, and both sides knew it was the best they could get.

'Good. I'll send a police car over to the TV centre to get you here as soon as possible so we can check the arrangements before the call comes in.'

'What do you make of it?' Mallory asked Fiona as two technicians worked in the background setting up the communications equipment.

'I'm not a happy bunny.'

'Why? Because you believe she's manoeuvred you into a position where she can use you in some way?'

'Oh, no, not that. I'm sure she does want to use me; I'll take that as a given.'

'Then what's the problem?'

'The problem is why she wants me there at all. Debbie's planning something, we know that. And it looks as if she wants the media on board by giving an interview to Mary Franklin. Fair enough, that will give her what she wants: attention and notoriety. But I still don't understand why she wants me there.'

'I'll pass on that one.' Falcon shrugged. 'But there's another question that bothers me. And this is a strictly practical one. She wants to be interviewed over the phone by Mary Franklin, and that will take time, so we should be able to locate her position.'

'And that's a problem?' Fiona sounded puzzled.

'Connelly, like most of the population, has learned from TV police dramas that phone calls can be traced. So she must realize there's every chance we'll be able to pinpoint her location.'

'I see what you mean. Another enigma,' Fiona said. 'Why should she knowingly set herself up?'

'We can only wait and see. We'll put in place the tech team to pinpoint the origin of the call, and Sergeant Maltravers can run the communications from here. And I'll take Dan Logan off the watch on the portacabin and put him on standby with an armed unit and a dog team to pick her up if we locate her. But, like you say, she's no fool, and I can't help thinking it's not going to be that simple.'

48

Mary Franklin was in her mid-twenties, dressed casually in jeans and a denim shirt. As soon as she'd arrived Falcon had taken her through the communications set-up, explaining that when Debbie Connelly came on line her voice would be relayed over the speaker system and that the entire interview would be recorded. Two microphones had been plugged into the phone console, with a swivel chair in front of each one. As a media reporter, Mary Franklin was familiar with the electronics involved in modern communications and she was comfortable with the arrangements that had been made.

Now everyone stood around, making desultory small talk as they waited for the call.

At half past ten on the dot, the phone rang and Fiona and Mary Franklin took their places at the microphones. Goldilocks was sitting in front of a communications console and she threw two switches and made a signal with her hand for Mary Franklin to go ahead.

The reporter switched on her microphone. 'Mary Franklin.' Her voice was clipped and professional.

'Hi, this is Debbie Connelly.'

'Good evening, Debbie.'

'Have you made all the arrangements?'

'Yes, everything's set up.'

'And the police psychiatrist is there?'

Fiona switched on her microphone. 'Yes, I'm here, Debbie. This is Fiona Nightingale. We met before, you remember.'

'I remember.' There was something in the voice. What was it, Fiona wondered, knowing it could be important in setting the parameters for what was to follow. It sounded almost like suppressed aggression. But why?

Mary Franklin consulted a set of prepared questions on a computer print-out and spoke into her microphone again.

'Debbie, did you want this interview set up so you could tell us something? So you could deliver a message?'

'I wanted people to know I was the strong one.'

'You mean you wanted them to know you dominated Mark DeMasters?' Fiona came in, being deliberately confrontational.

'Hah.' There was an explosion of air, clearly audible over the speakers. 'Little Miss trick-cyclist. Your questions are *so* predictable, aren't they?'

'Have you been involved with psychiatrists before then, Debbie?' Fiona knew the answer; she was simply probing for an opening.

'Have I been involved with psychiatrists before? Only most of my life. Ever since I was in senior school.'

'Have they helped you?' Fiona was trying to sense how Debbie Connelly wanted the interview to proceed and Mary Franklin was content to let her make the early running.

'Helped me?' The tone was there again. And this time Fiona could identify it. Animosity. Open animosity.

'No, they have never fucking helped me. Not with any of their twisted theories. Not with any of their probing into my mind. None of it helped. Never.'

'Debbie, did you like it when you were in senior school?'

'Like it?' She seemed intent on repeating the questions. 'No, I didn't bloody like it. Too many pupils.'

'But were you a star in junior school?'

'Yes, I was always the one the teachers asked when they wanted something special.'

'And it was different when you moved up?'

'At first it was, yes.'

'What do you mean, at first?'

'Until I joined an after-school drama group.'

'And did people take notice of you then?'

195

'Too right, they did.'

'What was it like? Being centre stage like that.'

'It was great. Up there, you didn't have to worry about what was happening in every-day life.'

'But Debbie, it was all make-believe, wasn't it?'

No answer.

'Was there anything else about being on the stage in front of an audience?'

'Power.' Another voice this time, the words spat out. Mary Franklin jerked her head back instinctively, but Fiona held her ground.

'Power.' Fiona probed for an opening. 'Why is it important to have power?'

'Are you for real? It's important because with power you're strong. You're someone then, and you gain respect.'

Fiona sensed that they were getting very close to the heart of Debbie's problems now.

'So you became an actress when you left school.'

'Yes.'

Goldilocks lifted her hand in a pre-arranged signal to indicate that Debbie Connelly's location had been pinpointed. Mallory acknowledged, and put his mouth close to Fiona's ear.

'Keep her talking,' he whispered.

Fiona nodded. 'Were you a good actress?' It was time to start really challenging her.

'I could have been. But none of those dickhead directors could see what was in front of their eyes.'

'Did that make you feel you were a failure?' There were dangers in the question, Fiona knew, but it was a risk she had to take if she was to move the interview to another level.

'Listen to the bitch. You are so not right.'

'Were you a failure?' Fiona repeated the question.

'No, I wasn't a failure. I wasn't.'

The other voice, the angry words snarled out again.

'But you were a failure, weren't you?' Fiona decided to play her ace and stay on the attack. 'What about the play in Plymouth?'

A sharp intake of breath. Followed by a long silence, drawn out until Fiona thought she'd lost her.

'I don't want to talk about that.' The reply when it finally came was subdued, as if she was tired. And the aggressive personality had disappeared.

'Debbie, did you ask for this interview so that you could explain that you were the one driving the God Slayer? To show that you controlled Mark DeMasters?'

'I encouraged him. That was all that was needed after his sister died. Who would have thought little Mark had a violent streak? And all I had to do was unleash it.'

'But why? Why did you want the religious leaders dead?'

'I didn't particularly. I was just helping Mark.'

'No, you weren't. You were in the driving seat.' Fiona forced the issue. 'You helped him plan the murders so you could come to us later and pretend to be helping the police. Putting you centre stage.'

'I don't believe it.' Debbie Connelly gave a high-pitched shriek of derision. 'For once, just once, the bitch has got it right. Yes, I used, Mark. He was putty in my hands. At first we were all just good friends helping each other through troubled times. Me, Seb and Mark. But then Mark's sister killed herself and he wanted revenge.'

'And that was when you took over?'

'Yes.'

'And all the time you were planning to hijack the opening ceremony of the conference.'

'Oh, you're so clever.'

Fiona suddenly felt afraid. This was getting personal. And she realized then that it had been personal ever since the interview started. It was just the two of them. The *patient* and the *psychiatrist*.

And Fiona knew then why Debbie wanted her there. Because to Debbie, she had come to represent all the doctors who had ever interfered in her life and she wanted revenge for what they'd done to her. But what form was that revenge to take?

'What now, Debbie?'

'Now you start being afraid.'

'Afraid of what?'

'Afraid of what I will do next'

'We know you planned a finale on the cathedral steps involving

Mark playing the part of a dragon. He told us as much.'

'Yes, and with the right choreography it would have been a great piece of theatre.'

'But you dumped him, didn't you, Debbie? So what are you going to do next?'

'Oh, yes, like I'd tell you. But I can make you a promise.'

There was a silence, drawn out as Fiona waited. Then, dragging out the moment dramatically, Debbie Connelly delivered her shock.

'It will involve you and me. Just the two of us, Fiona, babe. Oh, yes, and all the thousands of people watching.'

Debbie Connelly had issued the threat. At that point she broke off the interview.

49

Before anyone could react, Goldilocks held up her hand and listened to a transmission in her earphones. Then she turned to Mallory.

'That was the leader of the phone tracking team with an up-date. Debbie Connelly's call came from the vicinity of woodlands near to the village of Langley – the place where we found the old chapel. DI Logan's team's on the way by helicopter, eta any time now.'

'See if you can contact DI Logan.'

'Will do. She flicked a switch on the communications console. 'DI Logan from operations room.'

'Logan.' The voice flooded into the room.

'Mallory. Dan, can you give us a status report, please?'

'We've got the location of the call now. It was made from the old chapel where Sebastian Banks was killed.'

'Are you ready to go in?'

'We are now, but it wasn't so easy. When it was built the chapel was designed as a place of sanctuary, and there's a stone on the path leading up to it that can be dropped. It's hidden and our guys didn't see it last time round, but it's a big stone and it must have been counter-balanced in some way because it seems Debbie Connelly moved it. The helicopter went down to the village and we collected ropes and ladders, and we've just bridged the gap in the path. We're moving into the chapel now.'

There was silence as the team moved in to secure the building, and it was a few minutes before Logan came back on the line.

'Sorry for the delay, but the place was in darkness.'

'Did you locate Connelly?' Mallory could hardly contain his impatience.

'Negative. What we found was a passage from the chapel leading out onto the rocks. Another safeguard that must have been built into the place by the monks. I'm afraid she was long gone by the time we got here. The chopper's scanning the surrounding area, and I suggest we intensify the search by putting more officers on the ground. But for now, it looks like Debbie Connelly's done a runner.'

Mallory shook his head. 'She's on the loose again. So where the hell are we now?' For a moment he let his frustration show.

'One thing has become clear,' Fiona said, 'She effectively challenged me to a head on clash. A personal duel, if you like.'

'Why should she do that?' Falcon asked.

'Quite simple, really.' Fiona sighed. 'As far as she's concerned I represent every psychiatrist she's had to suffer in her life. And she wants revenge. Boy, does she want revenge. And it will be public, you can count on that, because she talked about the thousands of people who'll be watching. And she's been smart because she's already got the media on board through Mary. So she's calling the tune, no doubt about it.'

'Hell.' Mary Franklin sounded as if she couldn't believe her luck. 'What an exclusive.'

Mallory nodded, knowing he was trapped and trying to find a way out. 'You'll get your exclusive, no problem. You were present at the interview when Connelly challenged Fiona and you'll have your copy of the tape, as agreed. And that puts you so far ahead of the opposition they won't even be in sight. But if you agree to keep everything under wraps until Connelly makes her next move, we'll let you be present at police HQ and watch the way the investigation develops.'

'How will it work?'

'We'll assign a member of the press office to be your liaison, and they'll walk you through everything. That means you're kept in the loop. It doesn't mean you're actually present during briefing sessions, or any other type of meeting. Deal?'

'Deal,' Mary Franklin agreed at once. After all, she told herself, she had nothing to lose. She'd already been present at the interview and now she would be able to use that as background to weave in the climax of the story: the duel between Debbie Connelly and Fiona Nightingale.

Goldilocks took Mary Franklin to the press office to set up the details of the deal. When they'd gone Mallory, Falcon and Fiona were left at the long table; an island of quiet now in the busy major operations room.

'I do not like to be beholden to a reporter,' Mallory said. He was obviously angry, but he had it under control now. 'But I think we've contained her the best way we can. And now we come to the real problem: Connelly wants some kind of showdown with you, Fiona. I want to make one thing absolutely clear; we do not, and I mean *not*, put any of our officers, and that includes you, in danger just to fulfil the fantasies of a deranged madwoman. She may be the ringmaster but we do not jump to her bidding in some kind of media circus. Agreed?'

'Yes, guv,' Falcon nodded.

'So what have we got that might give us an insight into her next move.'

'Not a great deal,' Fiona admitted. 'But there is one thing, and this is very important. She planned a public suicide at the end of the mystery play. True, she switched horses in mid stream and turned to the Guardians to offer them a deal that excluded Mark DeMasters, but I think her new plan will still involve ritual suicide. And in that case, she won't be too bothered about her own safety. So let's summarize.'

She began, to count on her fingers. 'One, we can be certain that whatever she has in mind will take place at the opening ceremony of the Faith Conference in front of the thousands of people she mentioned. Two, it will be spectacular. She's not come this far to go out with a whimper, and with the murders already committed she's already shown us that she's capable of staging an event. Three, she seems to want a contest with me.'

'What kind of a contest do you think she has in mind?' Mallory asked.

Fiona was quiet for a moment, thinking. In the end she shook her head. 'I really don't know, I'm afraid.'

'What does all this say about her mental state?' Falcon asked, pushing the questions along a new track.

'For years she's been an attention seeker,' Fiona replied. 'Why? To put it simply, because something in her make-up means that she doubts her own self-worth. In other words, she has zero self-confidence. Then she found the perfect solution. Acting. She could immerse herself in parts on the stage and to all intents and purposes, actually become someone else. The problem seemed to be, however, that she was OK in school plays, but she was never really any good as a professional actress. And the last straw was the review of the play in Plymouth, which effectively killed off any chance of her having an acting career. I really can't overestimate the damage that review would have had on Debbie. It shattered her world, and from her behaviour since then I would say she's losing touch with reality. Even to the extent that she's prepared to take her own life.'

Fiona broke off as Mary Franklin came hurrying in with her minder from the press office in tow.

'I've just had a call from Debbie Connelly on my mobile. Apparently, she wants me to be at the opening ceremony of the conference with a TV camera operator. Once there, she'll tell me what to do using mobiles.'

'So she's confirmed it is the opening ceremony that she intends to hit.' Mallory sighed, and began to pace the floor again. 'Do we take her on, or do we cancel the ceremony for safety reasons?'

'One thing,' Fiona stressed, 'We're dealing with a very dangerous psychopath here. And one who doesn't care what happens to her any more.'

Mallory nodded. 'I'll make all this very clear to the senior management group. They're already in session waiting for a briefing from me on the events of the evening.'

'So what will you tell them, guv.' Falcon asked.

'There are going to be kids swarming around all parts of the opening ceremony. And according to Fiona, Debbie Connelly's lost all touch with reality. So, until she's in custody, I can't guarantee the safety of the public.'

*

When Mallory returned fifteen minutes later he looked grim.

'The Guardians have had word from America. *The Breastplate of Judgement* is to be displayed at the opening ceremony of the Faith Conference, before being taken to Jerusalem where it will be given a permanent home. But showing it at Garton will be one of the media events of the decade and the decision of the SMG is that there can be no question of cancelling the opening ceremony now. Garton will be in front of the world media, and we can't be seen kowtowing to a single madwoman.'

'So what exactly do they intend to do at the ceremony?' Fiona asked.

'They liaised with the organizing committee, and it was decided to slot an extra item into the programme. A Jewish children's choir will be allocated a space in front of the Catholic cathedral, and they will sing as the breastplate is revealed to the public. This will take place on a platform that's already in place for Adam and Eve to play the Garden of Eden scene.'

'What about Superintendent Casterly? He's running security, so he's the officer at the centre of all this. Where does he stand?' Falcon asked.

'Ah, yes, Superintendent Casterly.' Mallory shook his head. 'It would seem he regards running the security at the conference as a major career step. He's carried out a full risk assessment, and he was able to convince the SMG that the risk posed by Debbie Connelly was manageable. In other words, he's guaranteed security for the opening ceremony. He was very persuasive and the SMG were happy to take his word for it, although I expect it was because he was telling them what they wanted to hear.'

'But you made your objections clear?' Falcon asked.

'Very clear. As did the deputy chief constable. But the SMG were equally clear. There's too much hanging on this and, in the absence of any compelling new evidence, the opening ceremony goes ahead. Warts and all.'

50

Short of cancelling the event, everything had been done to make the security around the opening ceremony watertight. The problem was, as Falcon remarked to Fiona, with crowds like this around and a multitude of individual festivities, 'watertight security' was more or less a meaningless concept.

In the pre-ceremony briefing, Mallory had left the overall security to Superintendent Casterly, although he'd added a few extras himself. These included placing an additional dog team and two armed units as back-up in the streets surrounding the cathedrals. He'd also increased the helicopter cover in the sky over the event. Finally, he'd set-up a 'state of the art' CCTV unit, with cameras covering all parts of the area involved in the ceremony. The unit was based in the mobile operations centre caravan, where two officers continually monitored a bank of TV screens.

Once he'd done all he possibly could to cover every contingency, Mallory had decided to concentrate on the single lead they had that could take them to Debbie Connelly.

Mary Franklin.

Debbie Connelly had asked her to be at the ceremony with a cameraman on hand, and be ready to respond to a mobile phone message. Mallory had put Mary and the cameraman in an unmarked police car close to the Roman Catholic cathedral where the culmination of the opening ceremony was to take place. Two motor cycle officers, and one of the armed response unit units were on stand-by next to the car.

Everything that could be done had been done.

But the tension in the caravan, that was parked in a side street halfway along the parade route, was rising by the minute as the time for the ceremony to start approached.

The centrepiece of the opening ceremony was a parade marching along the street leading from the Anglican to the Roman Catholic cathedral. The parade itself consisted of a colourful mix of marchers, dancers, bands, static displays on lorries, and street theatre. And the climax was to be the mystery play originally directed by Debbie Connelly. The players would act out the St George and the Dragon story in front of the audience and the choirs who were gathered under the dome of a huge canopy.

Mallory had set up a dedicated monitoring unit under the command of Dan Logan to check every move made by the players taking part in the mystery play, and to keep the play itself under surveillance once the parade started.

As the officers and technicians in the mobile operations centre waited there was a sudden burst of static over the radio. Sergeant Maltravers, designated Control, was sitting at a console with another officer by her side to act as an instantaneous back-up if called upon. Goldilocks leaned forward and adjusted the volume as the transmission came over the speakers.

'Zulu One to Control.' Logan's voice came over the net.

'Control. Go ahead, Zulu One.'

'The parade has started.'

'Control. Thank you, Zulu One. We have it on camera. Keep us informed of any developments.'

'Zulu One. Nothing suspicious so far. Repeat, nothing suspicious.'

'Control. Thank you, Zulu One.'

'Zulu Two to control.' Another voice came over the net.

'Control. Go ahead, Zulu Two.'

For the next few minutes reports came in as the parade moved along the street. The tension in the operations centre continued to build.

'Remind me,' Mallory asked Superintendent Casterly, 'What happens when the ceremony's over.'

'The people taking part in the parade move into the car-park at the rear of the cathedral. From there, they disperse in their own time. All except the actors in the mystery play. They stop on the cathedral steps and perform a final scene on the Garden of Eden theme where Adam and Eve eat the forbidden fruit. It's a story that's common to the three major religions, and at the end the actors playing Adam and Eve are taken up by a glass lift to a model of a tree on a platform above the cathedral steps. Once they're in place on the platform, the breastplate is unveiled and a Jewish children's choir sings on the steps. Then the ceremony is brought to a close. Quite a spectacle really.'

Mallory looked at Superintendent Casterly. 'And I hope that's all it is. A public spectacle.'

For a moment Casterly blanched, only too aware that it was largely on his say so that the ceremony had been allowed to go ahead.

'Zulu One to Control,' Logan's voice cut in.

'Control. Go ahead, Zulu One.'

'The mystery play has reached the cathedral steps and is about to start acting out the scene with George and the Dragon.'

'Control to Zulu One. Keep Control updated on progress.'

For the next few minutes Dan Logan gave a running commentary on what was happening.

Then another voice came over the net, this one from the car containing Mary Franklin. 'Zulu Three to Control.'

'Go ahead, Zulu Three.'

'Target has not made contact with Mary Franklin. Repeat, no contact yet.'

'Thank you, Zulu Three.'

'Zulu Two to Control.' There was an edge of excitement in the voice.

'Go ahead, Zulu Two.'

'One of our officers has reported finding a semi-naked female body in the bushes behind one of the portacabins. Wait.' There was a short silence then the voice came over the net again.

'The body is that of PC Hardcastle.'

'Control to Zulu Two. Condition?'

'Zulu Two to Control. She is unconscious from a blow to the side of the head, and the paramedics are checking her out now.'

'Control to Zulu Two, has her radio been taken?'

'Zulu Two to Control, affirmative on that.'

'So there's an officer down and a female officer's uniform and radio missing.' Mallory cursed under his breath, then turned to Goldilocks. 'Warn everyone on the net that there's a rogue woman officer on the loose out there. Then request all, repeat all, female officers to gather by the main entrance to the car-park. Whether Debbie Connelly knows how to work the radio or not, we can flush her out this way, because she either joins the others and risks being recognized, or stands out like a sore thumb if she remains in the body of the car-park.'

When Goldilocks had relayed the order, Mallory took over the mike.

'Control to Zulu Two. Shut off all exits and entrances to the car-park.'

'Zulu Two to Control. Will do, but it's chaos here with everyone milling around; we request extra back-up.'

Mallory snapped out a series of orders, then told Zulu Two the extra back-up was on its way, eta in two minutes.

'Zulu Three to Control.'

'Control. Go ahead, Zulu Three.'

'Suspect has made contact with Mary Franklin.'

'Control. What was the message, Zulu Three?'

'Mary Franklin and the cameraman are to get as close as they can to the top of the cathedral steps and wait there.'

'Control to Zulu Three. Move Mary Franklin and the cameraman to the steps, but keep them under escort. Repeat, keep them under escort.'

It was unfolding now and the net was drawing around Debbie Connelly.

51

'Where is she?' Mallory spoke softly to himself.

'She's dressed as a policewoman, and that'll give her authority with the public.' Falcon was thinking out loud. 'But it will also increase the chances of being picked up because we're isolating all the female officers. So what will she do?'

'Sir, over here.' One of the officers manning the bank of CCTV screens called out, and pointed to a screen displaying the area around the glass elevator that was to take Adam and Eve to the platform above.

The screen showed a male officer standing at the top of the steps leading to the entrance to the lift. As he stood there he was approached by a female officer holding a child by the hand. As she started to climb the steps, the male officer said something to her, but she shook her head and pointed to the child.

'Can you zoom in for us?' Falcon asked.

The operator made a number of adjustments and focused on the woman's face.

'It's Debbie Connelly.'

Falcon turned to Goldilocks who had taken over Control again. 'Get the armed response unit to the base of the elevator. It might scare the kid, but better that than leaving it in the hands of a madwoman.'

But they were too late. Before Goldilocks could get the message out, Debbie Connelly suddenly rushed forward and kicked the male officer to the side of the steps. The move caught him completely by surprise, and for a long moment he swayed from side to side and tried to grab the safety rail as he fought to regain his balance. But she kicked out at him again, and he cartwheeled over the rail and fell into the well below.

Debbie Connelly positioned the child so that the little girl was trapped against the door of the elevator, then she quickly pulled off the jacket and skirt of the police uniform and tossed them to the side. Underneath she was wearing a long white dress, trimmed with gold ribbon.

Still holding the child, she moved forward and pressed one of the buttons on a control panel by the side of the elevator. The door opened and they stepped inside. The crowd in front of the cathedral gasped as the elevator began to rise. Mary Franklin talked into her microphone as the camera rolled.

'What's up there as well as the tree?' Mallory asked Superintendent Casterly, as the scene on the cathedral steps was relayed to the TV monitors in the operations centre.

The superintendent was visibly shaken by the turn of events, but he forced himself to concentrate. 'The lift stops at the platform that runs across the front of the cathedral on either side of the tree. That's where Adam and Eve were to act out the Garden of Eden scene. The only other thing up there is a synthesizer unit to provide sound effects as Adam and Eve symbolically eat the fruit of the tree and a children's choir on the steps sings.'

'Then what the hell does Connelly expect to do?' Mallory asked. 'OK, she's centre stage, and she has a big audience here, and a truly massive one with all the media that's present. But I repeat, what does she intend to do?'

'Just a second,' Falcon interrupted. 'Like you say, guv, Debbie Connelly's already got the audience. So why does she need Mary Franklin there?'

'Her own private reporter,' Fiona replied, 'To record what she's doing for posterity.'

'The synthesizer?' Falcon cut in. 'Who operates it?'

'A sound engineer,' Casterly answered.

'Is he up there now?'

'Yes. He went up earlier so as not to spoil the image when Adam and Eve ascend to the tree.'

'How did she get the child to go with her?' Fiona asked.

'Trust.' Falcon replied. 'Maybe she was lost, or just hanging about. But it doesn't matter because she would have trusted a policewoman. And now we've got a hostage situation.'

Mallory turned to Falcon. 'Take over Control. Tell the armed response unit to stand down temporarily. Then clear the car-park. Everyone out through the rear exit. Once the area's clear, bring back the armed response unit and prime the sniper to await orders. Everything's changed now; if the little girl's shown to be in danger I want to be ready to take out Connelly if I have to.'

Falcon moved to the console and sat down beside Goldilocks. 'I'm taking command.'

'You have command,' Goldilocks acknowledged.

Falcon started to issue a stream of orders. As he did so the people in the operations centre heard another gasp as the lift started down with someone in it.

'The sound engineer.' Superintendent Casterly looked at the close-up image on one of the screens.

'She's cleared the decks, he must have jumped at the chance to get away,' Mallory said.

A sudden burst of high-pitched sound crashed out. A screeching, resonating blast of power that seemed to make the air shake even in the operations centre.

But the sound was concentrated where the loudspeakers had been set-up on the steps of the cathedral. There, in the dome of the canopy the sound was trapped as wave after wave of noise echoed in the confined space.

The children started to scream, hands held tightly over their ears. Already the panic had taken over and a riot threatened.

52

The sound stopped as abruptly as it had started, and for a moment an unnatural silence descended on the area around the cathedral. Then it was broken as the children began to scream.

'Listen to me.' The voice of Debbie Connelly cut through the chaos as the teachers struggled to keep the children under some semblance of control.

'That was just to shock you and I will use it again if anyone tries to leave. You will all stay here and watch the spectacle. And what a spectacle it will be, ladies and gentlemen. Something for your education, delectation and entertainment.'

'It's a parody of the words used by the master of ceremonies in the old music halls.' Fiona found she was whispering. 'She's introducing the show.'

'Bloody hell,' Mallory cursed. 'Talk about a captive audience. No question, she's the centre of attention now.'

'So what about the show? What have I got planned for your entertainment? Wait and see. But I promise you, the little children will be safe. If my instructions are followed, that is. So, what do I want? I want the police shrink, Dr Fiona Nightingale, to come up in the lift and join me. And if she refuses, then I'm afraid the child up here with me will fall off the platform.'

She lifted the child into the air above the edge of the platform and a sound, almost a growl, came from the crowd as they realized they were helpless to intervene.

'I have to go to her.' Fiona refused to think. Refused to give herself time to make a rational decision. Because she knew that if she thought about it, there was no way she would face that madwoman on the high platform.

'No.' Mallory was adamant. 'We can't send you up there alone.'

'Like I have a choice?' Fiona didn't want any argument, afraid that her resolve might fail her. 'If I refuse, Debbie Connelly throws the child over the platform rail, and does God knows what permanent damage to the little ones on the ground with the sound blast. You think I could live with that?'

Mallory looked at her. She was angry and afraid, and it showed. But behind all that he detected a determination. But he wasn't about to give in easily. 'In your opinion, is Debbie Connelly completely over the edge of sanity?'

'Yes.' Fiona sighed. 'Her life's fallen apart now. Completely. Oh, she's in control of what's happening here. At this minute. In fact, she's making it happen. The ringmaster directing the show. But as far as reality goes, she lost that some time ago.'

'And you believe that she's prepared to kill the child she's got up there?'

'Yes, I do. If she doesn't get her own way.'

'Why does she want you there with her on the platform?'

'I still believe she sees me as some kind of sacrifice to satisfy the wrongs that all the psychiatrists have done to her in the past.'

'And?'

'And she might want to kill me. Or, she might just want to humiliate me in front of an audience.'

'Your best guess?'

'Depends if she lets me talk to her. If I can get through to her she'll draw the proceedings out, and maybe she'll settle for humiliation. But don't take bets on it.'

'But if you can start a dialogue, there's a chance you'll be able to talk her down, and safeguard the hostage?' Mallory wanted to be clear on that.

'Possible.'

'Then we have to try that without you going onto the platform with her. Ideas?' Mallory asked.

'She is presumably using the sound console to talk to her audience. But we have control of it because we can switch off the power.'

'Hold it there,' Fiona came in. 'That is one very dangerous strategy. If Debbie thinks she's lost her audience, it's all over for her. And she would be so angry that she could do anything. We simply can't risk the child's safety.'

'I agree,' Falcon said. 'But because we are *able* to switch off the power gives us a hold over her. A negotiating point.'

'And what exactly would we negotiate?' Mallory asked.

'The way in which Fiona talks to her. We could agree that Fiona takes the lift, but that it stops halfway up. Then Connelly stays on the platform and says what she has to say to Fiona, who remains in the lift. And don't forget, if that happens one of the snipers might get a clear shot at the target.'

'Fiona?' Mallory looked at her. 'We don't believe Debbie Connelly is armed, but if this goes ahead you would have to wear full body armour. The lift will be immobilized at the halfway point, so she can't bring you up to the platform. You'll have a crash helmet with built-in throat mike strong enough for the sound to reach Connelly on the platform. And snipers will cover the platform in case she attempts to harm the child. No time for detailed planning, so it's not perfect. But there's a young child being held hostage out there. And her life might just depend on it working.'

53

Fiona felt the bulk of the Kevlar body armour under her anorak. Even though Debbie Connelly was not considered to offer a physical threat, the vest Fiona was wearing offered the highest category of protection against stab and slash wounds. And bullets. Mallory had insisted she wore the protection, together with the crash helmet and built-in speaker.

She waited in front of the door to the lift as a technician from the company which was organizing the ceremony explained that once she was inside she could operate the push button controls, but that now the elevator had been programmed to stop halfway to the platform and not to go any further.

'Control to Gatekeeper.' Fiona heard Goldilocks inside her helmet, and realized the sergeant must have taken over the control again.

'Gatekeeper. Go ahead, Control.' The technician replied.

'Control, status, please.'

'Gatekeeper. Everything is in place.'

'Control, Fiona, you can enter the lift now. Good luck.' Clipped, professional words from Sergeant Maltravers.

Fiona stepped onto the metal floor of the lift, looked around once, then pressed the button labelled *Platform*. The door sealed with a swishing noise and the lift started to rise.

She looked outside at the view as it rose, and felt a stab of apprehension as she seemed to be suspended in the air. Then it came to rest. Silence. All around, wrapping the elevator in a cocoon. Suspended somewhere over a void.

Fiona shook her head to break the uneasy patterns stabbing at her mind. She wasn't especially afraid of heights, but the sense of isolation made her lose her bearings and for a moment she felt an attack of sickness. But it passed, and she reached up and slid back a panel in the glass roof.

She flicked one of the switches on her throat mike, said a brief prayer, then spoke.

'Debbie, can you hear me?'

'I can hear you, bitch.'

Fiona didn't need the equipment in the helmet to pick up her voice, the synthesizer mike she was using projected the words down to the crowds below.

Fiona's strategy was simple. Engage with Debbie and try to establish some kind of rapport that might lead to the release of the hostage.

'Debbie, you said you wanted to talk to me. Well, I'm here now. So, can you let the little girl go free?'

'And let the police shoot up the platform? In your dreams.'

'OK, Debbie, let's talk this through.' Fiona kept her voice soft, non-threatening.

'*Let's talk this through.*' The voice was a parody of Fiona's. 'How many times have I heard that? Winging, winging, fucking shrinks. But none of them understood.'

'What didn't they understand, Debbie?'

No answer at first. Then the words were snarled out. 'They didn't understand that I was special.'

'How were you special?'

'I had the gift, but none of those shrinks understood.'

Fiona was desperately trying to dig out a fragment of some almost forgotten memory. A patient she'd read about somewhere. Then it came to her. She hadn't read it in one of the professional journals, it was a patient who had been discussed among the staff at the clinic where she'd worked in New England. A young woman about Debbie's age had killed her parents because they'd failed to recognize their daughter's 'gift'.

Her gift as an artist.

Fiona remembered that the young woman had been in art

college, but had been rejected as having no talent. Was there a parallel here with Debbie Connelly's failure as an actress?

'The gift, Debbie; was it the gift of acting? Did it mean you could transform yourself on the stage? Touch people's imagination and carry them on a journey?'

'Yes.' There was a note of surprise in Debbie's voice. 'How do you know that? No one else did.'

Was there the beginnings of a rapport there now, Fiona wondered? 'Sometimes it's difficult to get talent recognized.' She played for time as she tried to drag up more of the memories.

What was it, one of the psychiatrists in New England had said? 'The patient's problem was really one of identity. Who she actually was. But she lacked real confidence in herself, and the gift, the painting, had been the one thing that had defined her. Or so she thought. She had been good at art in childhood, and later some of the promise had appeared to flourish in her teens. But in the end, it had all been illusory as the gift failed her.'

'The acting gift you have, Debbie, does it ever let you down?'

'You know about that?' Again, surprise in the tone of voice.

Quickly Fiona ran the options through her mind. She was sure she was just starting to peel away a single, outer layer, of her personality. Normally, she would proceed slowly, teasing out each stage in the personality analysis, but there was no time for any of that here.

The reaction when the New England patient had failed to attract attention through her art was that she turned to more personal forms of self display to earn recognition. Dressing weirdly, even shocking people by running around naked in public. And when that failed her as well, when her demons demanded more, she had killed her parents.

The common factor here was that both young women had gifts when they were children that had failed them in later life. Most people got over it, but for some it was a shock they couldn't live with.

Fiona knew then that what she'd failed to spot earlier wasn't the degree to which Debbie's attention-seeking had ruled her life: it was what she had been driven to when her gift was withdrawn –

when she found out that becoming a famous actress was no more than a dream, or worse, an unattainable illusion.

'Debbie, why don't you let the little girl go? We can still talk.'

'It's too late.' When the answer came the words were soft, and the voice carried a note of sadness.

'What do you mean, too late?'

'I was a good actress. People should have seen that. I was good.'

'So what went wrong?'

Silence.

'*I'll tell you what went wrong.*' The voice changed suddenly, the words screamed out now. '*It was all the fault of the psychiatrists messing with my head.*'

Silence again.

'*The fucking shrinks who thought they knew it all. But the boot's on the other foot now, isn't it? And you'll pay for what you did. You and the rest of the shrinks.*'

Suddenly, there was a scraping noise, and when Fiona looked up she felt an icicle of fear drive everything else from her mind.

She realized then what Debbie Connelly had planned. The past was the past. End of.

All she wanted now, was revenge.

54

'Message from SkyBird,' Goldilocks called to Mallory. 'Activity on the platform. Target's dragging something heavy along the floor.'

'What is it?'

'Control to Skybird. Can you identify the object?'

'Skybird to Control. Object identified as a sandbag.'

'Bloody hell.' Mallory's gaze was fixed on the wall running along the front of the platform. A shape had begun to appear on the top of the wall, manoeuvred into position by someone hidden from sight. 'She's going to drop the sandbag onto the lift.'

'Get the lift down. *Now*. And get a paramedic to the site.' Mallory snapped out, and Goldilocks relayed it to the team on the ground.

'Where did she get the sandbag from?'

'A couple of them were used to hold down the sound console table,' Superintendent Casterly answered.

'Come *on*.' Falcon was watching the elevator, willing it to start the descent, and as if in response to his prayers, it began to come down.

But it was too late; at that moment Debbie Connelly raised the heavy sandbag into place and pushed it over the edge of the platform.

'Whoops.' The high-pitched voice giggled in a grotesque parody of a small child.

For a long moment the sandbag seemed to hang in the air. Then it dropped, gathering momentum and hitting the top of the lift with a sickening thud.

Despite being made of strengthened glass, the impact of the

heavy sandbag cracked a corner of the lift roof and splintered one of the side panels. The impact drove long shards of glass into the cab and, as Falcon watched, one of them sliced into Fiona's leg, and a jet of blood shot into the air smearing the glass around her bright red.

'An artery's been hit.' Falcon struggled to keep calm.

Fiona was in shock. Her body was trembling and her eyes were starting to roll.

'Fiona,' Falcon spoke over the net, 'listen to me. It's vital that you stay awake. So talk to me.'

There was no reply.

'Fiona, we're getting help to you. How badly are you hurt?'

'Hurt?' She hadn't thought of that. Was she hurt? She saw the blood then, and somewhere in the back of her mind an alarm bell started to ring. It was her blood and the voice was right. She must not fall asleep.

For some reason that was important.

She forced herself to stay awake and ripped off her anorak. She twisted it into a ball and pressed it against the torn blood vessel. Like that, she managed to contain much of the blood flow as she shrank into a corner of the lift.

'Fiona, you've done well. Very well. But you must stay awake. Talk to me.'

Nothing.

Then a transmission came in, and Goldilocks turned to Falcon.

'The lift's jammed. The impact from the sandbag twisted everything out of kilter.'

Falcon cursed. 'Clear the area and bring up a fire appliance. When they can elevate the ladder, get them to approach the elevator and bring Fiona off. Keep the armed response unit in place, with orders to take out Connelly if they get a clear sighting. She's too dangerous now, but stress that the hostage is still up there.'

Goldilocks fired off the orders.

'Get SkyBird to locate positions of hostage and target.' Falcon was watching the platform through binoculars.

Goldilocks flicked a switch and sent out the request to the circling helicopter.

'SkyBird to Control. Hostage is sitting on the floor, tied to the sound console. Target is crouched in top right-hand corner of platform.'

Not for the first time Falcon felt himself wishing they had a sniper in the helicopter. They did have a special team of armed officers with helicopter training as part of a Home Office anti-terrorist programme, but they were all away on an exercise.

'Fiona, can you hear me?' Falcon spoke into the microphone calmly.

Something was there. Something in her head.

'What?' She had to force the word out.

Falcon breathed a sigh of relief. She was still with them. But he knew he had to keep her awake.

'You know you're ruining a perfectly good police anorak, and I had to sign for it?'

'On your money, you can afford it.'

She was responding.

'Target moving.' Goldilocks relayed the message from the helicopter. 'Crawling back to sound console.'

The updates were coming out like sound bites.

'Target dragging second sandbag from console. Moving along floor to far end of platform. Starting to lift sandbag onto edge of parapet.'

As she passed in and out of conscious from the loss of blood, Fiona was barely aware of what was happening. Then she heard another voice.

'Are you sitting comfortably? Oh, no, you're not, are you? I forgot. You're dangling among broken glass fifty feet in the air. I'm sure you know it might break apart any time. And you'd go fall-ll-ll-ll-ing through the air.'

As if on cue, there was a crunching sound and the elevator slumped to one side, grinding slivers of broken glass against each other and opening up more cuts in Fiona's skin. Then a long sharp sliver swung close, twisting around until it came to rest across her face and swung gently from side to side.

She heard another voice then. Screaming over and over again.

And she knew it was her own voice as she watched Debbie Connelly lift the sandbag for the last few inches and drop it over the edge of the platform.

It hit the top of the lift and the whole structure splintered apart in a shower of shiny glass shards.

As it did so, there was a long blast on a trumpet from the sound synthesizer and a figure in a white robe suddenly appeared on the edge of the parapet. Spreading her arms wide, as if she was delivering a message to the crowd below, she paused. Then she took a cigarette lighter from a pocket in the robe, snapped it on, and went up in a burst of flame. For a moment she paused, before spreading her arms again and hurling herself gracefully into space.

Debbie Connelly was committing ritual suicide.

EPILOGUE

'How's Fiona?'

'I'm in close contact with the hospital. She's still in intensive care, but she's stable now and her injuries are no longer thought to be life threatening.'

The deputy chief constable nodded. 'Too close for comfort though. She could easily have been killed. And Connelly?'

Mallory shrugged. 'The firemen caught her in the safety net they had in place for Fiona. She's got some minor injuries and a few bruises, and she sustained serious facial burns.'

'Will she face charges over her part in the murders and her attack on Fiona?'

'I doubt it. My guess is that they'll find her unfit to plead and she'll be put away for a long time in a special hospital.'

For a moment a silence hung between them, each man lost in his own thoughts.

'How have they taken everything upstairs on Executive Row?' Mallory broke the silence.

'It brought a few issues into focus, and the wolves are at the door already. For one thing, what happened today played right into the chief constable's hands by bringing the role of the senior management group into question.'

Mallory was about to ask something, but the DCC stopped him. 'Your position is quite safe. You were the one who advised that the opening ceremony at the conference be postponed until Debbie Connelly was in custody. And that's a matter of record. And I agreed with you, but we were outvoted and as chairman of the SMG I had to go along with the majority *view. In the end, no one was killed as a result of the decision, but we provided a spectacle of the worst kind for the world's media. There's no doubt now that the wrong decision was taken, and the flak over spheres of responsibility has only just started.'*

'Will this affect the changes you told me about last time we talked?'
Mallory asked.

'Oh, yes. Big time. It gives the chief constable the perfect excuse to launch his position paper.'

'Remind me, what was it called?'

'The New Face of Modern Policing in the Urban Environment - Responding to Changes in the Community.'

'Management speak.' Mallory grimaced.

'True, but I think you'll find the appointment of Paul Minton as ACC will be speeded up. And, once he's on side, the chief constable will move forward with his plans to give more power to the mayor's office and to the community at large. Things will, as they say, be a'changing. So, we need the "old guard" to stop the worse excesses, David. More than ever now.'

Light and darkness. Pain and relief.

The world was changing all the time as she drifted in and out of consciousness. Once, she thought she saw Lance looking down at her, then holding her hand. She tried to smile at him, but he receded back into the void before she had the chance. Another time she thought she heard voices somewhere in the distance, but in her drugged state she couldn't make out the words.

Then something altered. A new kind of vision was trying to enter her mind. Something from the far edge of her consciousness. For some reason she didn't understand she was fighting the vision, straining to prevent it moving in.

But she was too weak, and she felt the barriers giving way.

There was a sense of water. Dark, stagnant water with the stench of rotting mud. She became aware of a row of arches standing out above the water. Then she was inside a passage. It was lit by torches set into recesses and there were rugs on the stone floor and pictures in heavy frames on the walls. A door at the far end of the passage was open and light flooded out.

Inside, the room was richly furnished. Deep-red curtains, patterned carpet, glistening chandeliers and ornate gilt furniture. In one corner of the room a woman was seated at a delicately carved desk, her back to the door. She was wearing a formal crinoline ball gown, with narrow waist and full skirt, the heavy fabric divided into large squares. Each square was cut into four red and green triangular sections by a yellow cross running diagonally from corner to corner. On her head was what looked from behind like a black shawl that fell below her shoulders.

She was bent forward over the desk, studying something laid out on the surface. As Fiona approached she saw it was a pack of cards. But it was no ordinary pack, and all the cards seemed to have coloured pictures on them. Then the woman turned her head.

And Fiona heard herself scream.

The woman's face was covered in a circle of black material, sinister eyes gazing out through narrow slits.

It ended then and Fiona was back in the world of changing perspectives. She was still on the edge of consciousness, but she could think more clearly now.

She ran the vision through her mind again, and couldn't help feeling there was something familiar about the woman in the mask. Then it came to her. It was the dress the woman was wearing. Fiona had seen it before. A woman wearing a similar dress was in an old etching in her grandmother's house. It was of a carnival scene from Venice that had been a present from Fiona's other grandmother, the Venetian contessa.

Fiona had never met her other grandmother. Apparently, she'd isolated herself from the rest of the family, although Fiona could never discover why. And now she'd had the vision with its thread back to Venice. Was there something hidden among her ancestors in that ancient dark Italian city? Something that had been allowed to enter her mind as a result of the accident?

The accident.

She was beginning to remember now.

And, as the memories came, she screamed, trapped again in the glass box suspended high above the ground.

Then Lance moved closer and took her hand again.